Rusty Bolt and New Hope

COLONIZING A SPECIAL NEW PLANET

R. EVANS PANSING

Order this book online at www.trafford.com
or email orders@trafford.com

Most Trafford titles are also available at major online book retailers.

A special thanks to my wife, Phyllis and uncle Darrell Cayton and also JIM Hansel
in Arkansas Darrell Cay ives that provided incentive to continue writing Especial
my wife Phyllis and uncle Darrell Cayton Also Jim Hansel in Arkansas.

Printed in the United States of America.

ISBN: 978-1-4269-5213-5 (sc)
ISBN: 978-1-4269-5214-2 (e)

Trafford rev. 04/18/2010

 www.trafford.com

North America & international
toll-free: 1 888 232 4444 (USA & Canada)
phone: 250 383 6864 ♦ fax: 812 355 4082

I wish to dedicate this book to all the folks that have made my life a very enjoyable one. A special thanks to Dick Francis the mystery writer that penned this advice to me: write for your own satifaction, not worrying about any negative comments from others. This book is just that.

Rusty Bolt and New Hope

Cast of Characters

1. Russell (Rusty) Bolton (Bolt)---Captain –Master Pilot of the Hope Merchant, , Mechanical engineer & a PH.D in Astrophysics, plus other degrees.

2. -Evelyn Nicely Bolton, wife of Rusty = Ensign, Clerical expertise, Scientific Probabilities, Loves to cook, a real chef, some medical training, Caring with investigating capabilities, Major degree in Constructional engineering A minor degree in Paleontology.

3. Joel Kerr (1) Co- pilot and first mate, Lieutenant commander- Agricultural science and biology. Jokester. Long time friend of Rusty.

4. Gloria Archer Kerr –wife of Joel, Ensign, close friend of Evelyn. Forensic science, Trained in sociology, jurisprudence. Loves animals

5. Dirkson (Dirk) Dare-Chemical and Mechanical Engineer plus some Archeological experience-First Lieutenant, Pale blue eyes, aquiline nose, intelligent,

large glasses, owl-like, strong and stocky, husband of Midge.

6   Midge Dare –Airman first class, Ensign –Geologist and Archaeologist, small, dark piercing eyes, dark eyebrows and hair, sturdy and solid of body.

7   Rexanne Wheeler M.D., Lieutenant Commander-Doctor of medicine, surgeon, Highly intelligent, Botanist, Pharmacologist. Wife of Rodney.

8   Rodney (Rod)Wheeler, Lieutenant Commander, Archeologist, Architect, a dig's master, serious about work, good looking wide smile large mustache, medium build. Husband of Rexanne.

9   Eryka Walther, wife of Sparks, meteorologist ,Ensign-Very Gregarious, climatology, TV beauty, thespian and accredited teacher.

10   Sebastian (Sparks,)Walther; First Class Lieutenant, Electrical engineering, communications expert , Computer genius.

11   Whisper Winslet , Daughter of Battle Winslet, Young, winsome, fair haired Nordic features, Blue eyes. Varied interests and degrees. (Pep, Whisper's faithful dog.)

12   Lambert Bright-(Bert) Brilliant young Captain of Comet Chaser II following Hope merchant. many scientific degrees and experiences. Very intelligent and gregarious.

13   MacPherson's Arch is the space arch that shortened intergalactic travel by bending space inexplicably. Founded by Evans MacPherson.

14   Garner Trapp- An associate with Lambert Bright, proficient in electronics.

15 Fairly Trapp, wife of Garner, Fair skinned, gregarious, Intelligent and accomplished in speech and communications.

16 Walter - On board Battle Winslet's ship, a helper of electronic and mechanic regulators. Walter in cabin two.(Wife Zoe)

17 Battle Winslet- High Counselor and Minister of defense and transportation. Father of Whisper & Waver, Short tempered, usually uncompromising and pertinacious.

18 Riley Striker Member of Lambert's crew Hardheaded, rank is First Lieutenant.

19 Bristle Fume Member of Lambert's crew, trouble maker, rank is lieutenant.

20 Bonnie Gale, the wife of Victor, one of the Commanders.

21 Universal Galactic Flight Academy.(UGFA), Galactic Exploration and search unit, (GES).

22 Carl, Battle's expert of plasma engines and repairs . (Wife Lovey)

23 Porc, a close friend of Waver.

24 Waver -Son Of Battle and Blenda, a ne'er-do well.

25 Blenda- Wife of Battle, compliant and wise. mother of Whisper and Waver.

26 Victor Gale-Lieutenant Commander comes to associate with Rusty's Group, wife Bonnie Gale .

PROLOGUE

The world was slowly dying. The oceans were so polluted that no eatable fish were existing in the waters. The populations had swelled to unsustainable numbers. Wars and conflicts were everywhere men wanted to live and raise animals or farm. The governments no longer could constrain the masses that wanted what others had. The vast majority of peoples were procreating at a faster rate than the infrastructure could accommodate. Many areas were now in the hands of families or clans that dictated the rule of law in that area. People were in a constant state of uncertainty that spawned terror and violence in the streets of many cities and towns. Only the strongest were in positions to maneuver around and formulate some answers to the universal problems. The men and women of the Universal Galactic Flight Academy and the Galactic Exploration and Search Unit tried to find ways to support this overstuffed planet by giving hope to the masses that colonization on other worlds was the answer. The space flyers had found no habitable planet so far and none in sight. All were in despair or discouragement, all but a few. Some saw hope in a insignificant report.

Rusty Bolt

CHAPTER ONE

When a person needs to be renewed or just pepped up it is a real challenge to get up and do something different. Doing something different means to get to second base you must first take your foot off of first base, a comfortable place, won and secure. Second base is an unknown.

The news was sketchy at best as well as unbelievable. The item was well back in the reports filed by The Galactic Exploration and Search Unit of the United Worlds Federation. The little paragraph stated that on one of the GES forays their search sensors picked up a celestial body that was more earth-like than most of all other discovered planets. It had an unusual feature in that it was not fully round-like as were other celestial bodies; an impossible occurrence stated the blurb. The sensors must be out of calibration or just incorrect the item declared. It ended by stating no further explorations or searches were to be made in that region because of its distance and the object's odd feature .

Rusty Bolt read and reread the item. It piqued his interest so deeply he finally spoke with himself. "This has to be the most interesting piece of news for our world that I have seen in years. Earth is so crowded that it cannot properly support itself as well as conflicts and wars are without number. If we can get to a world that size and shape we could colonize it and have a new sense of pioneer adventure to relieve the boredom here on earth. Also, many mistakes we have made on this planet could be avoided if we could start all over again. Equality and Freedom for everyone."

Rusty put down the report and just stared into space while mentally visualizing a new world to inhabit for the fearless and adventurous. He had a thought that the sky had a hole in it just for him to investigate. He would petition the GES for a permit and a vessel to extend the search for a new place for earth to colonize. It would be long and difficult at best, that is if he could persuade the powers that be, that a possible new world exists for humans. All of the planets found so far have been inhospitable or too small (moon-like) to support human life as we now know it. He must tell his good friend and sidekick of this challenge. Joel was just he type of fellow one would want on a long ride in space. Rusty narrowed his brow for a moment, realizing he would have to get married and so would Joel if this adventure meant actual recolonizing a new world.

Rusty knew his wife to-be would need the same adventurous spirit as he had. She would have to be someone willing to take risks, work hard and not be too fussy about appearances. A real friend and a friend to bend and weave as the conditions dictated. Bend and not break. A lass of rare beauty and fortitude.

Rusty was no prize winner himself. Six feet tall and two hundred pounds of muscles. Russet hair of an unruly nature that was spiky at best. His face was strong with freckles and with a smirky type of smile that bewildered all strangers and charmed his close friends. His brow was high and intelligent above a nose that was perfect in a Roman sort of way. Rusty carried himself in a manner that spoke of pride and accomplishment. Eyes that saw more than what he was looking at. Blue-green and penetrating. A man with tomorrow in his eyes and a fire in his belly. His schooling was numerous and varied so that he could converse with anyone about anything and be instructional as well as interesting. His most valuable assets were his twinkling, electric blue-green eyes and engaging smile of near perfect teeth. Many rare features but when consolidated he was just very common looking for a captain in the space navy. Rusty was certain he would find the perfect wife among his many friends and acquaintances. After all, he was a captain of the Galactic Pilots of Earth.

It might be more difficult for Joel because of his humorous nature and his ability to interject smart retorts to peoples comments. A quick wit was ingrained in the stocky man-boy. His frame was strong and steady with bulges of muscles all around. His hair was black as were his eyes that flashed and occasionally winked when he was in the center of conversation. Joel was very well educated also, in numerous sciences with degrees in many areas, similar to Rusty. Joel had a nice smile although it was usually surrounded by a day old stubble, black as night. His nose beamed crooked because of the many fights as a boxer at the Galactic Academy for pilots where he was graduated with a commission as a sub-captain.

Mr. Kerr and Mr. Bolton were both at a dance when they began to plan the trip. Their serious conversations attracted a young lady of their acquaintance. A Miss Eve Nicely also attended. Her beauty was famous throughout the assemblage. Rusty had always liked her for her wit and charm as well as her beauty. He thought she was too smart or complicated for him to try to date. He had been so busy in academia, that dating was not high on his agenda until now. But he asked her out anyway. To his surprise she said "yes." The dance turned into plans and flight possibilities. She fit right in and maintained the questioning conversation until it was shown that something about colonization was the gist of this planned flight.

Eve knew that the earth was so over crowded that it was only a few years from some type of annihilation. Millions were already starving and the conflicts between the have-nots with the haves had reached intolerable proportions. Food was always scarce as people had settled on the choicest pieces of land to set up tents or hovels to eke out an existence. In many places disease tried to even out the great numbers, but scientific advances had kept complete devastation at bay. Eve was tired of pushing through crowds and throngs and seeing it only getting worse. She fell right into the boys plans by saying;

"Well, me buckos, this seems like a plan that I have been thinking about for some time. I hope you can count me in. We have been told by the authorities that no planet has been found to support life as we now know it. Resulting in that no deeper space probes would be allowed." Eve commented even after only sketchy information.

"Well, Eve that has been true. Joel and I hope to petition the powers that-be to give us one last chance. Our main point will be that human existence will soon be snuffed out if another probe for recolonization is not tried. We think a small party of young people could travel the distance and then explore and repopulate the planet in question as well as notifying earth that there is a place fit for habitation and re-population. Maybe in time we could establish agricultural areas and send back to earth in big freighters the results of that endeavor." Rusty finished by looking straight into the eyes of Eve with new hope in his heart. She could be the one.

The formulating of plans and the completion of permits and grants for the mission seemed to Rusty to be without end. The governments had so many forms and inquiries that had to be handed from one lackey to another paper pusher on into infinitum. The process appeared to be a runaround instead of just plain ineptness. Many old timers wanted to stamp the journey as an exercise in futility since most of the exploring by them had resulted in negative results. Rusty and Joel went to all of the agencies with a persistence and convictions that must have eventually convinced the old sages to grant permits and funds to sanction the expedition with a host of conditions and exceptions for the crew. It was with some official hesitation that all of the required conditions were met by Rusty and Joel.

During this interval of time both pilots began to court prospective spouses as well as the permitted accompaniment of scientists that would travel with the expedition.

Joel had found a young woman that appealed to his sense of adventure and mirth. Her name was Gloria Archer.

Rusty and Eve had found common ground for a lasting friendship. Both couples doubled dated frequently and found to their mutual future happiness that matrimony was being seriously discussed by both couples. The real content of the expedition's destination was not revealed in any clear form to the girls or anyone else. Just a survey for possible colony sites. This was the scenario given to everyone because of the apparent need for secrecy. The complete revealing would come as Rusty and Joel were settled about the girl's commitment which was more than evident in all of their conversations and hints with Eve and Gloria. They each had no qualms about their new found loves. It was just a precaution that the authorities had demanded the boys to take with everyone. Too much revelation resulting in jealousies might crop up its ugly head where it didn't belong. The girls were more than convinced of the excursion's purpose when Rusty and Joel began to recruit a crew that included all married couples with extensive backgrounds in geology, engineering, archaeolgy, medicine, mechanics, climatology, electronics and communications. Eight sciences, five couples, added up to a serious expedition.

Eventually the two boys popped the questions and were blessed with ardent and enthusiastic answers in the positive. The marriages took place at the academy chapel with a host of friends and families in attendance. Even the new crew members had been invited to their multiple joy. Now we had five couples going somewhere together for some special reason thought all of the chosen few. The ceremony was spectacular as pictures were taken, and good food enjoyed. Many questions were posed by family and friends alike to the consternation of the fortunate crew. They gave truthful but brief answers because they knew very little about their new assignments anyhow. Rusty and Joel were still tight lipped, evading or revealing any pertinent information." We are going on a flight to just look again at possible places for colonization." After all of the festivities were exhausted, the bridal parties left for a few days of anticipated honeymoons.

After a short time away from the crowds and crush of people the newlyweds returned to the task assigned to them, briefing the other crew members. The four newlyweds had been sequestered on one of the governments last remaining unoccupied pieces of real estate. It was a real treat not to have to deal with crowds and discontented people of all walks of life. Hunger and disease were still on the rise.

One of the latest reports disclosed that a large contingent of people was beginning to colonize even the Antarctica. A terrible place at best to live and raise a family with only the barest of comforts and necessities. The report said they were living in tents and shacks of an assorted mishmash of material. The logistics omitted by the squatters were so great that only a few would be alive when winter descended on them.

Rusty was able to secure the remaining permits and documents to lift off in a matter of days. Joel had informed all, that a closed meeting would be held Monday and all would be revealed at that time. The first order of business was to reintroduce each other in a more detailed fashion than they had originally. Each couple stood and gave a thumbnail sketch of their life experiences and special talents.

The first member was Dirk Dare, a young man of flawless qualifications with the sheer look of intelligence. A high brow and aquiline nose. Pale blue eyes of the altruistic variety that went with someone very flexible and kind. His forte was chemical engineering and with a background that had him involved in government work as well as university research. His wife rose up to add to the information about this married couple. Married now three years with no children, thus far. Her specialty was geology. She had participated in explorations all around the globe before marrying Dirk. Now she was considered an impeccable expert on earth strata and minerals etc. Her name was Midge. A small girl, close to the ground for intense observations and discovery. She had dark piercing eyes with dark eyebrows that were on the heavy side for a young girl. Her most startling feature was her gregarious nature and her infectious giggles.

The next couple to tell about themselves were a physician and an archaeologist. The doctor's name was Rexanne, and she was very qualified in her art, from simple trauma to complicated surgery. Her husband the archaeologist was well versed in all kinds of past civilizations. Rod Wheeler was one of the world's great archaeologists. Rexanne Wheeler basked in the glow of her husband's related exploits. Rod was a physical man but with glasses and the look of academia. A man with a wide smile but no nonsense when his digs were involved. His nature was calm and cool. Rodney was a good looking dude even with his ample mustache.

The last couple were both congenial and outgoing. One could tell by their smiles and eyes. They were people that had risen above the average with grace and beauty, coming from very poor and disadvantaged backgrounds. Climatology and electrical engineering of communications would be well attended to by these two knowledgeable people. Eryka Walther and her husband Sebastian Walther, who was known by his nickname, Sparks, filled the compliment of knowledge and camaraderie that would be needed on this long and exhaustive trip. The Walther's had spent a lot of time on ships at sea and in the space universe travel, giving valuable expertise as well as thespian talents when requested. They also had some experience in TV as well as other forms of telecommunications, some so new only a few knew of there existence. Eryka was a beauty that graced many screens as a climatology and weather expert. Sebastian was an electrical engineer and computer wizard.

At last, Rusty in strained humility gave his degrees and credentials with the vocal corrections by his new found love, Evie. Rusty had piloted many kinds of space craft being proficient under a variety of conditions. His degrees being in astrophysics and mechanical engineering. He had been to deep outer space numerous times.

"Some of which he would not like to recall in detail," Evie chided her new husband.

She continued with soft but with accurate verbiage concerning her own talents and background.

"Most of my education has been in probabilities and clerical proficiency as well as statistics. My forte is keeping records and documenting events. I have been known for being nosy when trying to get at facts. So please disregard or forgive me for asking so many questions, seeking facts and information. I also love to cook. and hope for good things to come. Being a chef with wide experience, I know I will compensate for any inconveniences I might cause you."

Rusty beamed with pride and satisfaction as he then introduced Joel Kerr and his wife, Gloria. Joel divulged his duty as copilot and first mate of the trip. His degrees were in agriculture and biology. A special combination of sciences. Two fields of science that would benefit a mission such as this. Gloria was not one to be out done by all her new husband's talents. She declared with a humble type of flair she had degrees in Sociology and Forensic Sciences and a minor in Universal Jurisprudence.

When all had seated themselves, Rusty was very glad that he had also run all of the names through the Academy's computer bank (clandestinely) for abilities as well as compatibility studies. Psychological profiles were very important, Rusty thought, as he scanned the room for any evidence of negativity. The process had brought together a group of people that would benefit mankind when and if any inhabitable planet could be located after so many failures.

Rusty continued with a voice that demanded attention and exuded confidence.

"One of the deepest probes and scans of late has given me the impression that a medium planet near a medium sun has indicated the possibility of habitation. Not seen or verified but the probe's sensors gave some real positive indications that It was out there on the fringes of the universe. Many galaxies away from here. Why it has not been detected before must be that its light signature probably gave a distorted image. We have been given one of the finest retrofitted freighter spacecraft known and now a crew to match. I had to convince many an ear as well as twist a few arms to secure such a space vehicle. We have been in the inception process for many weeks. I ask all of you to keep the goal confidential so that no one in this crowded planet will cause us to delay or miss this chance. The window of opportunity is so very narrow."

Rusty knew quite well that no secret was totally safe at the space port but any effort would be appreciated so that a minimal number of people would be aware of the saving feature of the mission. The in depth revelation of a mission to recolonize on an earth-type planet class could cause world wide chaos. The Captain continued. "We lift off in three days so tell your families and friends of your flight but not its goal. We are just looking for distant planets. The next two days we will all familiarize ourselves with the duties, the design and construction of the space craft. For your information the name of our ship has been commissioned, HOPE MERCHANT."

Rusty finally gave the 'you may be excused,' order so that the group formed little knots of conversation. Rusty looked out over his crew with satisfaction and pride. They all looked so formal and official in their new gray and red uniforms that would be quickly shed once they were in hyperspace. Each member would stand out in any crowd with red piping and red insignias complete with shoulder boards decorated with ranks rounded out the handsome uniforms. Rusty was a captain, and Joel was a sub-captain, but now a lieutenant commander for this flight, most of the others were lieutenants and the two new brides were ensigns Most designations would be soon disregarded on the new planet, thought Rusty. Rexanne was a lieutenant commander as was Rod. All navy and flight trained as well as their chosen professions at the Universal Galactic Flight Academy. Complete with uniforms the group would have at least two days of shakedown before engaging the ionic plasma drive and hyperdrive complexes; they would launch into space reaching out to the timesaving MacPherson's arch. Even with these time and recent scientific advantages the voyage would take about one year to travel. That was if no unforeseen difficulties arose. Something that was just as certain as smooth sailing and unvarying sunsets, thought Captain Bolt.

Rusty Bolt

CHAPTER TWO

The two-day shake down cruise went without a hitch. The crew familiarized themselves with all aspects of the ship. The Hope Merchant was a refitted freighter with some battle armaments and new power drives. The ship was large and spacious. Besides, all the necessary equipment needed for exploration on land, Rusty had requisitioned some animals. A very small flock of chickens, a pair of rabbits, and a pair of small goats. He had wanted big pigs but settled for two of a variety that was quite small. No beeves because of size. The crew would take turns caring for the animals not to be eaten but for their colony, when found. Large water purification units and aqua collectors for gathering water and recycling it. Compartments for food of all kinds and varieties to satisfy any palate. The ship had every kind of convenience for a long trip. A laundry, multimedia room,, exercise facilities, workshops for repairs and personal pastimes. A small room had been set aside for haircuts or beauty treatments, if so desired. Rusty had not wanted a brig but the old freighter had one that was still there where it had been before the retrofit. When going through the ship, Rusty had delegated each section to one of the crewmembers to keep in order and oversee any needs (including security) for that area.

The two days of shake down went flawlessly and all were anxious to get under way. Just before Rusty was going to enter hyperspace, Sparks called on the com system to alert Rusty of an important message coming from Academy and Spaceport headquarters for his ears only. Rusty made a beeline to Sparks com room and began to adjust the dials plus the various configurations for optimal transmission. Rusty entered his codes as Sparks left the room. The base began its transmission.

"This is base commander, Admiral Joshua Smidely. "We have received a report from our computer department that its personnel files have in some way been tampered with. This leaves us to believe that someone in your crew may not be who they say they are. We have no specific proof of this, but it does present a problem. Our investigation is on going. We will leave any decisions in this matter entirely up to you, Captain Bolton. I would be most careful in your dealings with the crew and document any unusual circumstances. My recommendation , but not an order is for you to return to base until all is cleared up. If you need, any further assistance or aid of any kind please notify us before entering hyperspace." Admiral Smidely. signing off."

Rusty was concerned but not discouraged by this bit of news. The Admiral was not absolutely positive that the tampered computer files were about his crew and not some personnel on base. Rusty was not without quilt as he had roamed the computer without permission to get information on all of his present crew. The best thing to do, thought Rusty was to only tell Joel and maybe our wives to be on the lookout for any suspicious activity that they might notice.

Returning to the cockpit and captain's duties, Rusty gave no countenance that would support anything serious or of an unusual consequences of the Admiral's message to the crew. And of course, no one asked about it or its contents, the result of a dedicated, disciplined, crew.

All members of the Hope Merchant crew reported that each station of responsibility was ready and able to jump into hyperspace. With that information and with all controls programmed for the jump along MacPherson's Arch. Rusty hit the appropriate red buttons for the leap into a place of mystery and wonder. The white star lines passing outside the ship's windows gave the confirmation of super speed. The mysterious MacPherson's arch gave the advantage of arriving at a destination in a time continuum that still puzzled science. The planned destination would still take at least a year even on the Arch. Super speed initiated the effect that was one of tingling about the body and a giddy sensation that each felt in a slightly different fashion, for only a moment.

The crew all seemed to be in a good timbre as the first of many meetings were called by the Captain.

Rusty began with a slight deviation. "The base contacted us about the possibility of a computer glitch. I would like everyone to run diagnostics on any computers in your area and report back to me when finished. Are there any questions you might have that you would like to ask me now?"

Joel spoke up first to sort of break the ice. "What's for dinner and who is cooking?"

A controlled laugh was vented by the group. It broke the ice.

The group was advised of the occasional possibility of going into a state of being that permitted a body to be in suspended animation. Each crew member had their own body cabinet with recalculated information for a successful hibernation. Only recently retrofitted to their unique personal specifications. This was for rest and refreshment for the body, soul and spirit. The box or cabinet is designed to be filled with inert gases, and the temperature lowered to near absolute minus zero where molecules came to a near halt. All life essences would be carried by initializing intravenous pumps to facilitate all essential body functions before the deep freeze. A procedure used many times for long space flights to alleviate boredom and curb any possible aging fluctuations. Up to five members could sleep at one time. These sleep times would not be regular but would be determined by the captain when he decided it was needed for the health and well being of the crew. The first shift would be by lot, the only exception being that either Rusty or Joel would have to be on the awake team and not participate in the lottery. It was decided by acclimation that Joel would sleep first with four others and Rusty would sleep in the second shift when or if it was necessary. 'It was nice and unexpected that all was going so smoothly,' thought Captain Bolt.

The galley was filled with activity the first earth night. The crew all accepted the standard time frame that would stay with them throughout the journey. Earth days and hours etc. would be their reference of existence until they arrived at their destination.

Supper was concocted by Evie Bolt and Midge Dare. The arrangement was by mutual consent and was a culinary success. Applause and cheers were the order on the meal as they all knew that this kind of gathering would be infrequent and rare at best, for a long time. Most meals after this one would be nutrient wafers, concentrates, and microwaved food stuff, unless the two cooks opted to cook for the crew. After coffee and some exotic teas, the duty roster was posted for the next day.

Rusty took the lead by announcing, "get a good night's sleep for tomorrow we will fall into a monotonous routine for the next year or so. We have a very important mission to perform for all mankind, and it will take everyone's skill and dedication"

"We have drawn lots for the first group to deep sleep time and reassigned duplicated duties for the remaining crew members. I have cautioned each sleep member not to take books to read in hibernation or snacks," said Joel with a twinkle in his eyes.

A muffled snore of chortles greeted Joel's dry humor. The gathering broke as though by some unseen magnet pulling each couple to their respective cabins. All the cabins were similar except the captain's. Rusty and Evie had a slightly larger cabin that contained two desks rather than one and had extra room for charts and monitoring devices for the ships progress. Many books were in evidence as was vision monitors for messages and entertainment viewing. Large double bed, dresser, a snack bar, closets and a spacious head or bathroom gave the Bolts all that anyone could hope for on a long journey. Bolts is the preferred name of the Captain and his wife after the marriage.

Both of the Bolts kept busy with reports and observations until late in the night. The room was filled with the anticipation of many days of togetherness for the newlyweds. In this context it was difficult for Rusty to begin a dialog that would dissolve this halcyon atmosphere for some time to come.

"Evie, I must tell you about the communiqué I received from base earlier today. Admiral Smidely. informed me that the base's computer files for personnel had been tampered with. The end result being we are to watch everyone that was selected by computer to be a possible threat to the mission. Joel knows about his and I am certain he will tell Gloria.

We are not to become paranoid about this event but only more diligent about security on board. I used that computer myself before the trip so I might be the one that base has detected as a hacker"

Evie looked quite surprised. " Naughty boy. Everyone seems so compatible and gregarious. It is hard to believe we have a possible saboteur on board."

"It doesn't have to be a saboteur; it might only be person's desire to leave the awful conditions on earth. If our true purpose were known by many, the lines of applicants would far exceed our ability to process them all."

"I still don't like it. For us to keep looking over our shoulders or suspecting our crew of devious activities. It just destroys the happiness and spirit of expectation making them null and void. Is it possible that we could sit down with each couple explaining our predicament and hope for some kind of revelation?"

"Your idea may be the best, but I think we will wait a little while before we show all our cards," summarized Rusty with a yawn of generous proportions.

In another cabin the Kerr's were having a similar discussion.

"Gloria, we can't just sit down everyone interrogating them to the point of tears or frustration trying determine which couple if any, might have altered the base's computers to get on board. It just doesn't make any sense to alter the personnel files to get on board when the qualifications would soon be discovered if they are not qualified. I think then they would fess up if confronted. I am certain Rusty won't allow it and will let things go on with the notion that any guilty parties will eventually expose themselves."

"I still don't like the whole thing and will be apprehensive until the truth is known," expressed Gloria with conviction in her voice as she continued to prepare for a night's normal but possible fitful sleep.

The ship was on auto pilot but Rusty had all of the ship's gauges and instrument monitors in his cabin to assure a monitored flight. Any difficulties were reveled by buzzers or beeps. Both Rusty and Evie were light sleepers so they both went to slumber land within minutes.

About 3 A.M. earth time, a soft buzzer sounded and wakened Rusty to examine the monitoring devices. A hatch door had opened on a lower deck in one of the storage rooms. When the camera showed only for an instant, the back of a moving object, Rusty hurriedly put on his clothes.

Evie sat up and asked, "what was the matter? Where are you going?"

Rusty was hard put to give a causal answer.

"A buzzer went off. I think it might be a malfunction, but I will have to investigate. You go back to sleep, and I will tell you all the details when I return."

Rusty left his cabin with a lump in his throat. That hatch door that buzzed was in one of the storage rooms that also led to the armory with guns and ammunition. The Armory room that was not to be opened or entered until they reached their destination. The Storage room was too close to guns and ammunition to dismiss the buzzer as a malfunction. Moving swiftly Rusty thought about getting Joel for back-up, but thought the lost time would be to his disadvantage. Moving swiftly down the passages he felt at his side his stun gun and was comforted.

CHAPTER THREE

Rusty moved down the passageway as he felt the hairs on the back of his neck raise. Rusty thought, 'There should be no one at this area except Joel and myself.' Moving closer to the storage door, Rusty took a defensive stance with his stun gun at the ready. Rusty, arriving at the door, found little evidence that the door had been opened or jimmied. Surveying the surroundings and finding nothing but some infinitesimal pry marks, Rusty gave a close examination of the door and lock. He found nothing indicating a successful entrance. The only thing left to do was to return to the cabin, reset the monitors and go back to sleep.

The night passed without any further interruptions. In the morning, the galley was filled with a hungry crew as Eve and Midge prepared a sumptuous breakfast. No mention of the armory's warning buzzer and subsequent search was forthcoming. The captain did explain a few more rules and guidelines that he had forgotten the day before. The sleep and subsequent order would take place whenever the captain decided boredom or stress had set in. In the meantime, each member would avail themselves in study, physical training, and reeducating themselves with the complexities of the ship's functions. On that point, the captain would have an examination in about three days. It would be in the spirit of friends and students all.

After breakfast, everyone returned to his or her areas of expertise or to the library. Dr. Roxanne Wheeler was very impressed with her surgery suite. The Wheeler's room was right next-door. Everything a doctor would need, even for the most complicated procedures. She took an exhaustive survey of meds and appliances. To her surprise, she found it to be different that the original catalog. Only a few mild pain relievers were missing. It was a small discrepancy but one never the less. Nothing very serious,' thought Rexanne, 'but it must be reported.'

Dirk Dare was in his lab making certain that all of his requested chemicals and lab-ware were registered and adequate for the job ahead. Some of the more dangerous chemicals were under lock and key and matched the original resister. The error was the missing of a small amount of sodium chloride, a most unusual occurrence. Dirk weighed the container and its contents that reaffirmed his original findings. Scratching his head, he debated whether to inform the Captain of this discrepancy or not. Finally, as Dirk pushed up his large spectacles he decided to report his findings to the Captain as he had been requested to do.

Rod Wheeler was in his little cubbyhole examining again all of the tools required of a successful dig. Brushes, trowels, screens, shovels, and many other required implements for his employment and joy. While Rod was humming and smiling to himself, an item caught him short on his list that was missing. It was there when he took the first audit; he was sure. 'Why would a small pry bar be missing?' Thought Rod as he cast an inquiring eye at the place the tool was supposed to be. "Certainly an omission that must be reported to the captain," said the big man with the droopy mustache to himself.

These three august and distinguished members reported to the Captain almost simultaneously. Each member on hearing the others relate their discrepancies in their respective areas of responsibilities began to advance theories for surely something was amiss. Rusty listened to each theory but did not reveal any of his. The meeting soon ran out of gas and dissipated to other areas where they were to keep quiet any negative comments about their dubious findings.

Rusty went to the cockpit and pilot's area. Joel was attending to minor adjustments and documenting the ship's progressive behavior.

"Joel, we have a bundle of unusual circumstances on board. I need your fresh and clever opinion about these events."

The captain related all of the reports he had just received and tried to present them in a manner that was casual and informal not putting emphasis on any points. The news was such that Joel finally stopped his duties to pay full attention to the captain. Rusty continued with an expressionless face.

"Each crew member seemed to think the errors were of a suspicious nature at best and not just clerical errors. My own opinion is I want to withhold the information for a later time. I am certain something fishy is going on. What do you make of it"?

"I don't like it a bit. I smell a rat or two that have a plan for sabotage as we go further into space for some nefarious reason. Do we have any cheese for bait to set out a trap or maybe a worm? These discrepancies noted are to our advantage and we better being doing something about it or have our heads examined."

Rusty braved a strained smile at his friend's comment. The Captain stood up and put on his most serious face as he addressed his second in command. "I quite agree and wanted your input before advancing any plan of exposure. I would like you to develop some kind of special detection in those areas that were specifically breached, without cheese. It may just be closing the barn door after the horse is out but to target all the areas might raise suspicions and alert the guilty."

Joel rubbed his eyes and drew his hands down over his face in a typical manner that expressed concern and weariness. "Horses, fish and rats aboard, this may be a job for an animal expert. I'll try my best to rig up some kind of detection device without raising any undue concern or suspicion. It won't be easy, as I'll have to be a magician to accomplish this chore. If you don't mind, I would like to inform Gloria of all these events. She is quite good at discovering any clues and it will give her something to do, keeping her from becoming bored."

"I am going to relate everything to Evie because of her analytical mind and level reasoning. Tell Gloria everything and ask her for her invaluable advice." With that comment, the two friends returned to their respective duties.

Eventually, Captain Bolt went to his cabin where he informed Evie of all the events recently transpired. Eve was most attentive and became engrossed in deep thought.

"What is the matter Eve?"

"I was just thinking about my own inventory of stock in the pantry. It appears we have lost a package of cheese and a box of crackers. Probably a clerical error. I didn't think it was such a big deal as the crew had access to the pantry. My thinking was that one of our crew just took them for a late night snack or to feed a need for comfort food between meals. Now, I am not so sure."

"Why."

Because the package was large. More than a snack.

"I think it needs investigating.

"You of course are right. It will bode us well if we not mention any of these episodes that could be bandied about in a conspiratorial manner. We will have our hands full with duties without adding some mysterious fodder to the mix. At best these are just coincidences and at worst a crewmember is causing us anxiety. Nothing yet damaging. I hope that we can eliminate any stowaway possibility as we searched all compartments twice before leaving as well as tight security when at the base. I am having Joel place some surveillance devices secretly at some strategic locations on the ship that will be going unnoticed, with or without cheese but should reveal our mischief-maker.

Evie looked at Rusty with questioning eyes as she said, what's this about cheese?

It was with gray and painful thinking; Rusty began to muse to himself about situations both here and back home. 'Why do people have to be so willing to make nefarious or painful activities their chief aim in life? So many want to follow a straight and narrow path in life while it takes only a few to sour its sweetness. The world we left behind was operating like a bunch of uncivilized miscreants. Every man for himself. The result, a dying planet. This mission is to give mankind a new hope that will present great new opportunities. Earth was filling up with no disciplines or self-denials. An orgy of over population and refuse accumulation. A nasty combination. To once again gain land and create visions of pioneering lost back on earth was Rusty's vision.' Coming back to today's realities, he concluded his mental dissertation.

"I now have enough evidence to suspect that someone has been making unusual interruptions concerning the mission and possible safety. Joel is to set traps without using cheese for our mystery instigator. I better get busy and do something before it gets out of hand."

RUSTY BOLT

CHAPTER FOUR

The days wore on with a kind of rapidity that surprised all members of the crew. No new or menacing activities were reported by anyone. Several members commented on some irregularities, all of which could be explained away as coincidences. A few mentioned some mysterious but unfounded occurrences. Maybe all of the crew was becoming paranoid. Joel had reported one sighting with his hidden cameras but assured Rusty it might have been one of our own people since no recognizable features were discerned. In addition, it had been during waking hours for the entire crew. Nighttime shenanigans were the rule.

During these beginning days, the impression came to Captain Bolt to reverse his earlier thinking about deep sleep requirements. All of his crew was so full of energy and enthusiasm he didn't think boredom would be an issue for quite sometime. In its stead he would at the first sign of any tedious repetitions of his people, he would pull out of hyperdrive and leave hyperspace for a time of reconnoitering and exploration to energize any tedium. The journey would take longer but maybe some valuable new information about the fourth quadrant could be learned. This would liven things up and maybe even put our skills to the test. Rusty's thinking came to sudden halt when Gloria and Eryka Walther came bounding into the cockpit with unified chatter.

"We have found more evidence of the sort that suggests that we have a stowaway on board."

"What have you discovered?"

"Reserve water bottles have come up missing. We were all told not to drink any of it until we reached our goal where it would be used in our forays into the new planet." Both women spoke by talking over each other as the news was spilled out.

"How about finding any empty bottles?" Asked the captain. "That might confirm your suspicions. Ask Dr. Wheeler if she might have appropriated some for her lab as a water that would be more pure and to her liking for medical purposes, superseding my earlier instructions." With those comments, the two ladies went to seek out Dr. Wheeler for an answer to the questions.

When they found Dr. Wheeler she was preparing Petrie dishes using freshly prepared agar. Dr. Wheeler related her faux pas to the two ladies asking questions.

"I just wanted to use the closest and most unalloyed water that was obtainable at the time. The ship's water is not suitable for my lab work. I am too used to just getting my own way as we doctors usually do. I am sorry if any permanent damage has been caused by my foible. Is there anything I can do to repair this breech of protocol?"

"We only needed to know how many bottles are missing. Do you remember how many you took?" Gloria spoke with only mild questioning; trying not to infer that it was no more than a nosy bookkeeping event inquiry. The doctor related that she was not certain because some water was placed in her sterilizer. She guessed the number at five or six but was not positive. She had discarded the empties in the waste compactor.

The two ladies took this news of unproductive value back to the captain. Rusty was not placated with the news. He was not able to have the entire crew on high security alert because of the stringent rules governing all their movements. That kind of edict would hamper all of the recent personality bonding of the crew.

Rusty's reply to the two inquiring ladies was short and to the point.

"Just keep this information or your unsupported findings to yourself. I hate secrets but occasionally it is needed. I'll look into any action to take that might be needed concerning the doctor and her faux pas involving the water misappropriation."

When Gloria and Eryka left the captain, he began to put on his worry face. Sparks Walther had earlier come to him to complain of a pair of headphones that had disappeared from his communications cubicle. They could be used to plug in and access all of the entertainment as well as ship's transmissions.

In addition, Joel had reported that another image had been caught on one of his hidden cameras. A rear shot of someone with the build of a female. Small with narrow shoulders and a feminine gait. A new and more comprehensible search must be made of the ship even if it's very immense size hampered a consummate detection.

The following day, Joel and Eryka Walther began a new search at the rear of the ship. Eryka volunteered to help with the care of the animals and was going to the rear of the ship so Joel went along for some security. They both walked along deck two in the aft section of the freighter. This deck contained lumber, pipes, electrical wire, cables, and even machinery for excavating and mining operations. All of these and more were stowed aboard the Hope Merchant to establish a new colony when and if the supposed medium planet were found.

At the end of the corridor, Eryka turned off to the right towards the animal holding area. Joel went straight on. Eryka was carrying some special food supplements for the goats, rabbits etc., so the heavy pail was taking all of her attention. Joel had gone farther along the passage and was engrossed in his inspection of some large fuel containers.

When Eryka had reached her animal responsibility, she was attacked from behind with ferocity and a shriek like a banshee. She fell forward with the result of hitting the deck with such a force that rendered her momentarily unconscious. She recovered quickly to find the pail of food supplements gone. Joel who came running back to see what the commotion was all about heard her scream and a shriek. She told Joel what had happened as she felt her head for the lump that was forming.

"What happened here and where is the animal supplement?"

"I was just slowly walking back to the animal pens when something jumped on my back and gave out a terrible cry of rage. I just seemed to fold up as the attacker jumped on my back. I blacked out for a second just before you came back"

"Well I will stay with you as we continue on to the animal compound so we can finish our chores. I am contacting Rusty about this incident on my com. unit. Let's keep our eyes and ears tuned for any other disturbances. I have my stun gun out and ready."

"Disturbances my foot. It was a full-blown attack on me, I lost my pail, and it's contents. Vitamins, minerals, molasses, mixed with rolled oats and wheat biscuits. A tasty meal for man or beast,"

"I am surprised you didn't catch that thing and put it in its place."

"Did you contact Captain Bolt about sealing off this section and send a search team to help us locate this bizarre enigma?"

"Not yet. I was too busy getting back to you when you screamed."

Joel took out his com-unit and related all to Rusty with the suggestion about sealing off this unit and sending a security team to investigate. The team came within minutes and worked out a plan to search the area by twos, in a crisscross pattern that would leave nowhere to hide. Joel was telling the team of the attack and to be ready for anything incase one of the larger animals had got free.

Dirk Dare and Evie Bolt went down the fuel passageway with drawn stun guns only to find it completely devoid of any anomaly. Returning to their starting point they noticed a huge packing crate that was unsealed. Upon closer inspection, they saw a piece of cloth protruding from the crate's seam. In unison, Dirk and Evie pulled on the crate's side. To their surprise, they discovered a young lady with her dog snarling in the corner of the huge container. The scene was complete with the pail and a half eaten chunk of cheese and a few water bottles.

With shouts of success by Evie, Joel came running to the crate with Eryka close behind. When Dirk and Evie revealed the unknown culprit, Joel took charge of the examination.

"All right, little lady. You and your nasty dog get out of that crate and bring the pail of supplements with you." Joel's voice was very stern but looking closely a twinkle of the eyes could be detected.

Joel asked the intruder, "what's your name little girl," as the dog made deep throated noises?

In a quiet, almost muted, or hushed response she replied, "Whisper"

Joel suggested they all wait to interrogate any further so that when Rusty questioned her; they would all gain the same information at the same time. Especially her name to be given in a normal voice.

The investigators all agreed at once.

The girl was about twenty years old and petite in stature. Blazing blue eyes and a shock of unruly blond hair gave her a certain Nordic look. Petite and yet muscular in a feminine body. Her dog was all black and more furry than hairy. She called him Pep and related to all that he was an Australian Canyon Jumping Kelpie of unusual intelligence. The dog seemed to be familiar with the passageway as he pulled on his leash as though he was expecting a filet mignon at the corridor's end

"Whoa little doggie. Not so fast. You'll get up to the captain soon enough," said Joel as he stooped down to the pet the dog's neck with a caring but manly scuffing. He continued, "Pep is certainly a friendly dog."

"Mister, he is only friendly when I tell him to be." The girl spoke with authority and conviction, in a husky but normal voice.

Within a few minutes, the entire group returned to the pilot's area and squeezed in to witness the questioning of the young lady. The air was tense with anticipation as Captain Bolt looked at her with penetrating eyes. The girl looked back with as good as she got.

"What's your name little lady."

Her answer was with audacity and conviction.

"If I told you, you wouldn't believe it"

All eyebrows rose up in surprise as Joel presented her purse.

He had removed it back at the crate and now gave it to Rusty. The questioning was going to be difficult, Rusty thought, as he opened the purse and looked at its contents.

RUSTY BOLT

CHAPTER FIVE

The captain opened the dainty little purse to reveal the girl's identification.

Rusty thought hard whether to reveal all the pertinent information at this time with so many onlookers. After an interval of a few minutes, he decided that all were entitled to this information.

"Her name is Whisper Winslet, no doubt the daughter of high counselor, Battle Winslet, the minister of defense and military transportation which includes our ship."

"Wow! How can we explain this to the higher ups?" Joel was quite taken back by this revelation. "I guess now, keeping her for a big ransom is out of the question." A bit of mirth that went over like a lead balloon.

"Even so my thinking is that old Battle might think we kidnapped his daughter. This turn of events might just get all of us in a peck of trouble with the Admiralty. Let's all get back to work people." The captain was very emphatic with his semi command. He rubbed his forehead as though trying to remove an invisible pain of ample proportions.

The group thinned out quickly without any murmuring or complaining. Then the pilothouse became much more conducive to personal questioning.

"All right Miss Winslet lets get down to the nitty gritty. Are our assumptions about your parentage correct? And why and how did you get on board this exploratory mission?"

"I got a space port pass from my Dad, so I just got aboard during a lapse of security. The mission's purpose was talked about at home and as it was becoming unbearable to live on earth with so many people crowding the cities and resorts, so it was natural to get on with space travel. The seas becoming polluted and everyone's nerves on edge, it just seemed the thing to do. I just found a big crate on this freighter, placed its contents in the back of the compartment, and moved in. Pep and I just appropriated necessaries, as we needed them. Sorry about the attack on the nice lady. Pep thought she was an intruder making his attack natural. I jumped on her to remove the dog with my usual command banshee yell. I just want to get somewhere where there is space and clean air. Even our oceans have become polluted. My field is anthropology, both cultural and physical as well as teaching. Those credentials on earth would give me little chance for adventure as well as advancement. The sciences and computer skills are the areas of the future unless one is exposed to a new world where teaching a new colony would be an adventure and a contribution to mankind. Some how I thought I could be an asset on a new colony."

"That's all well and good Miss Winslet. How about this envelope I found stuck in the back of your crate?" Joel then handed the brown and official looking envelope to the captain with a wink at Rusty.

"This presents a mystery to me, whisper. This envelope is an official communiqué from the Ministry that your father heads. How did you come to be in the possession of such a high level memo and do we dare to open it?"

Whisper put out her elfin chin and with her mouth, now a thin line, she began to reply to Captain Bolt.

"I heard all the information from my father and some of his closest advisors at home. They divulged information about the seriousness of the earth's condition without being aware I was eavesdropping. The future seemed so grim, causing me to want to leave. When they drafted a resolution about keeping your mission's purpose a secret, I purposed to leave even without the blessing of my father and mother. I also think it might contain some specifics that could be spurious or of a clandestine nature. They operated in a manner that suggests chicanery on the part of father and his cronies. I saw it and took the envelope so they would know some one else is aware of this draft. I don't know what it contains but you can open it if you want. I became intrigued with the idea of a new world that might lay out here just beyond the known space. That is why I came aboard to share in the adventure that awaits the venturesome."

"Well Miss Winslet, we can't turn back so we will make use of you and your talents some way or another. You have compromised the mission by your very presence. You should be thrown in the brig. Food and oxygen will have to be watched closely for we took on a very precise quantity of each and now must be adjusted accordingly. We don't even have a way to verify your claims and story, compromising security. We won't turn back and there is a chance your father may initiate some sort of search and rescue for you of a hurtful nature. For now, we will have to find space for you to bunk in. We have a small cabin we have been using for cleaning and maintenance supplies that you can clean out and move in. It will be enough for you. I assume you will care for and be responsible for the dog in the animal compartment."

"Yes captain, I will and what shall I call the others?"

"I'll give you a roster of names and will add your name before tomorrow. After a few more inquiries, that Joel will make then I will see what else we can do with you. You may retire to your quarters, as I must get back to my duties. Joel will show you the way to your new room. You will stay there until I call for you to associate with the others. Do you understand?"

"Yes I do and I hope I haven't caused any of you serious trouble."

With that response, Joel took the young lady to her new quarters to clean out and prepare for the journey ahead. He advised her that Pep would have to be placed in the rear of the ship with the other animals and Eryka or one of the crew would tend to the dog's needs.

Joel returned to the pilothouse after a few minutes where upon Rusty sought his advice about coming out of hyperspeed. Joel quickly agreed. Whereupon Rusty would have Sparks locate a communication buoy to send some messages back home.

"What kind of messages do you intend to send?"

"I feel we must inform Battle Winslet about his daughter's presence. Even a culpable father deserves to know were his daughter is."

"Aren't you concerned that we may get an order to return earth?"

Captain Bolt rubbed his chin and rolled his eyes as he said, "I feel certain that is just what will happen unless we transmit only and then garbled any response as we sign off to mask any base response. It may sound sophomoric at best but that is my plan. We can also take time to scan for anyone trying to follow us by our plasma signature. I get the sensation that we are part of a nefarious plan that we have not been apprised of."

"Sounds like a plan, cap. I will tell Sparks to try to locate a communication buoy in an area we can come out of hyperspeed on MacPherson's Arch. He will be glad to get an order that will challenge his skills as an electrical engineer. At that juncture we can scan for anyone trying to follow us and maybe they will pass on by."

Joel went to the communication center where Sebastian Walther (Sparks) was running some diagnostics with Eryka Walther helping her husband.

"Sparks, cap wants to locate a communication buoy out here when we come off MacPherson's arch, if you can, so we can send a message home. Let him know the calculations to come out of hyperspeed, ASAP. If I can be of any help just let me know."

"I can get that info for the captain in a little while," said Sparks with conviction and authority.

Sparks gave no indication that help would be required, so Joel gave a "see you later," and left the Com. Center. Returning to Rusty and aiding in the duty of flying the Hope Merchant. Settling into the co-pilots seat Joel began to think about the ships situation. As old friends, they talked about the mission and the possibility of a saboteur on board as they were attending to the many intricate and delicate systems.

"We might need to interview each member and quiz them about their qualifications as well as their resumes. I could give you three and I would take three. That way we might be able to flush out any possible counterfeits in the group. This would have to be done in such a manner that would keep them all imperturbable. Do you think we can pull this off as a part of an official procedure, Joel?"

"We can do anything, old cap, just like the old days."

Joel was probably referring to some academy shenanigans that had them call on all their skills to get out of tough spots.

About ten minutes later, Sparks called with the information that Rusty needed to come out of hyperspeed. The coordinates were such that Pilot and copilot began immediately to punch in numbers in the ships computer to accomplish the maneuver needed for reverting to sub light speed. Rusty punched the red enter button and the ship gave an imperceptible shudder as the star lines came back into focus. The crew had been notified of the change and begun to gather close to the pilothouse.

"Now what," said Rod Wheeler as he stroked his mustache and smiled a wide toothy smile?

'We must begin scan-sweeps for anyone following us as well as any anomalies that might require our discernment. I will compose a communication for Sparks to transmit later on. How far away is the buoy you have found, Sparks?" Rusty looked at Sparks with trusting competence.

"It is within a Cosmic Mega K but it will take several hours to relay, enough time to be on our way so that a trace will not locate the origins of the transmission."

"Eryka, you help your husband if needed, with his electronics. Evie will prepare a scrumptious meal while we are in sub light speed. Gloria you take meticulous notes on all our activities in your journal, while Dirk prepares any search, shuttle launches if required. Midge you gather any tools that might be needed if we make a foray to a nearby planet or moon. Doc you do the same, I have a feeling we will make some kind of a landing before we leave this sector. After all, a buoy was placed here sometime in the past for a reason. Rod you can use some of the tools needed for any exploration we might make. Midge you can also help

Rod with his diagnostic equipment for the possible shuttle launch. Joel and I will try to keep on top of all the activities as they unfold."

'These actions may let us know who is not who we think they are', thought captain Rusty Bolt as the crew moved towards their respective assignments.

Rusty Bolt

CHAPTER SIX

The pilothouse became very quiet as the crew moved away to fulfill the captain's orders. Only Joel remained with a look of admiration at his friend and captain. The two men had the trust and regard that had been built upon years of association. They had been friends since first school. Joel could have been commissioned a captain but had decided it would be to his advantage to take orders and not give them. Especially from Rusty Bolt. He now looked to Rusty for any last minute orders concerning the scan and possible shuttle launch.

"We will have to keep an eye on everyone to see if they fulfill their occupational skills. By the way, have you informed Miss Winslet that she could come out of her imposed isolation for these activities?"

"No cap. I had almost forgotten about our little stowaway. I will check on the little bird right a way and give her all the news about what is coming up. By the by, cap you know that her presence makes the crew an uneven number, sort of unlucky in the annals of flying of ships on the high seas of space exploration and all. You know, seven come eleven and all that stuff."

Joel left the pilot house with the vim and vigor that he was noted for, leaving a captain with worry lines starting to intrude upon his youthful brow.

Rusty was not superstitious but had doubts about the unexpected addition of Battle Winslet's daughter. The old man was noted for his tenacity, and his power plays at all levels of government. The message he was forming had to be very truthful but vague so as not to alarm anyone at base headquarters, especially Battle Winslet.

Rusty squinted at the words he was processing, as he looked up each word for its literal meaning on the computer. It had to be just right or there would be all blazes to pay. The words came slowly and painfully as he began to realize the whole mission could be dependent on this transmission. After an undetermined time and two cups of coffee later, captain Rusty Bolt headed for the communication' shack.

Rusty found Sparks and his wife still making scans to verify earlier results. Sparks was looking uneasy as Rusty entered the compartment and wondered what was the quandary.

"What's happening Sparks?" The comment by Captain Bolt gave Sparks a start and moved Eryka ever so quickly out of her seat to allow the captain a place to ensconce himself by Sparks.

Sparks was not perplexed but was caught in some activity not sanctioned by his Captain.

Rusty patted Sparks on the back as he handed Sparks his composed message to send back to headquarters.

"Oh, nothing too exciting. We are just verifying all of the readings we had earlier, and trying some new techniques to reach farther out for any other landing that might be partially able to support an investigating survey by us. I am just wondering if it would by in our best interest to try to land a shuttle craft on a moon with only a short time to explore a place that no doubt has been observed by others decades ago "

Just then Whisper was passing in the passage-way with Joel, she stuck her head into Sparks domain and suggested that if they were contacting her dad," just tell him I am safe, unharmed and happy. That should keep his blood pressure down."

Rusty was puzzled by her acrid remark so he addressed her in an authoritative manner.

"Miss Winslet, I opened the official memo you had in your possession. Do you know what it says?"

"No, not exactly but from the conversations Father had with some of his old cronies and his sense of self, I would wager it spelled out some nefarious scheme."

"Very true, miss Winslet. Your father's memo spelled out a plan to acquire with government funds several ships of the freighter class to transport high-ranking personnel and government lackeys to our destination planet to occupy and rule as kings. He feels certain the days of healthy, existence on earth is numbered as we do. But with one exception. We want a free and democratic colony with a constitution and by-laws that protect the weak and innocent. Sparks, when you are ready, I want you to send a short message as suggested by whisper. Whisper is found, unharmed and happy. We will include her in our roster of crew and participants of our mission. Sign off as Captain Russell Bolton of the Hope Merchant."

Sparks was relieved as was Joel and Eryka. Whisper also seemed to be very satisfied that the message would be transmitted much as she had suggested. A minor triumph for Whisper, now more mature than what her parents had pegged her. Especially her father. Whisper did not linger at the communications compartment but asked Joel if she could visit Pep. This request was accompanied by a command that she have Midge go with her as it was her turn to feed and care for all the animals.

Whisper found Midge, and together proceeded to the rear of the ship. Pep was overjoyed as the reunion was mixed with wagging tail and licking tongue. Whisper was also glad for the reunion as she cooed and whispered sweet words in the dog's ear. Meanwhile, Midge was busy with feed for the animals and making close observations of the mission's hope for meat on the new planet.

Midge said without really thinking," why were you named Whisper?"

The answer came with a sigh of benign annoyance.

"My mother is very diminutive, and father is a large man with a booming voice. To get my father to listen to her she whispers her conversations so father will be quiet and listen. When mother gave birth of me my father inferred I would be another whisperer. Therefore, they named me Whisper and have been wrong ever since unless the conversation is one of the more delicate kind. If you know what I mean."

Midge was satisfied with the answer and knew that the others had wanted to know and now she would be able to tell those that wondered about Whisper's name. The two ladies completed their mission and returned to the front of the ship where the cabins were located.

The shuttle excursion was to include the captain and 3 other crewmembers. Rod, Dirk and Midge, would make up the away team along with the captain. The little gaggle of scientists assembled themselves at the shuttle bay on the top deck. Each had brought a representative selection of tools that might be required on this expedition. As they assembled in the small cramped craft, Captain Rusty made an unusual change in plans. Coming out of the shuttle, he ordered Joel to take command of the mission.

"O.K. boss. I can handle this assignment with no sweat. Just let me go back and get a few essentials of mine and then we will be off."

Joel left when he got a nod of approval from the captain. The others made motions of stowing their gear and ensconced themselves in the craft's seats. There was a certain cramping of bodies and equipment noticed by Joel as he made his hasty return. Joel was able to squeeze by the others to purchase the pilot's seat next to where Rod had positioned himself in the copilot's seat. When all were belted in and settled, the shuttle's door was closed and secured by Rusty. The captain gave a slap on the craft and saluted as Joel fired up the engines and launched out into the deep and unknown.

Rusty was not able to explain to himself why he had made the sudden change of the shuttle's command, unless it might be that he wanted to be present if any scans or message transmissions needed his attention. He thought about all of his crew as well as the short time they had been on MacPherson's arch. This timing could merit a command to return to base because they hadn't even reached the place of no return. He knew it would take days to outfit a ship to travel so far into deep space. According to the memo, Rusty had intercepted from Whisper, old Battle Winslet might be ready in only a few days. Not enough time cushion to avoid the High Counselor in a race to the planet they were seeking. Maybe we could rest or hide on this moon that Joel is investigating and let Battle Winslet and his cronies just pass us in the night, as it were. It would be a good idea for me to interrogate Miss Whisper concerning her dad, and any idiosyncrasies he might possess. The old warrior must have some weaknesses, or flaws we could utilize. With these thoughts, the captain began to seek the vivacious miss Whisper Winslet.

Whisper was just finishing putting in order her ship's storage cabin. She had removed all the cleaning stores, and other maintenance supplies in a storage compartment close by. All of the material was stowed neatly and with some forethought of its future use. Captain Bolt approached her with a muffled cough to declare his presence. The girl turned around quickly and asked the captain if he needed anything, as though she knew he was in the vicinity.

"Why Miss Winslet, I would like to ask you some questions about your father, if you don't mind."

"Why would I mind? If you have questions about anything, I would be more than happy to supply answers to your queries." Whisper entered her room and indicated to the captain to be seated in one of two small chairs in her cabin.

"What exactly do you want to know about my father?"

"I was hoping to find a weakness of his that might indicate his reaction to you being on board this deep space exploration ship."

"The only weakness I can think of is his penchant to be first, be fastest and loudest at anything he does with little regard for consequences. He loves a fight and conquests. My mother may be the only weakness he has. She has been the moral force behind his rise to power. My brother Waver Winslet and I have never been close to father. Only mother has been able to influence any of father's unconventional behavior. Does that help you at all Captain Bolt?"

"I think that covers most of what I would like to know in case of difficulties from him at the earth base. Our plan is to not to respond or reply to our earlier transmission. We made it sound as though we tried but the transmission was garbled. In what way do you think that will affect your father when he tries to transmit an order to us?"

"Hard to tell. He won't like it and will try to blame or hurt somebody for the failure. He will strike out at what ever has caused this failure. That may be us, captain. He certainly has the ways and means to do it too."

Rusty left the girl's cabin with deep thoughts of concern. It was bad enough to fly into the unknown now there was added an old war horse who might be inflamed by the loss of a daughter than had suddenly grown up. It was time to check in with Sparks to see if any base headquarters had attempted replies. What we needed now was one more challenge to make this mission nearly impossible.

Sparks was just getting up from his seat when he saw the captain. His face had concern written all over it as he addressed his captain.

"Captain, we have just received a communication from base. I thought I would bring to you right away without even reading it in its entirety." Handing the message to Rusty, the electrical engineer hesitantly returned to his cubical.

Opening the communiqué, Rusty was seeing his own words fulfilled, right before his eyes.

Rusty Bolt

CHAPTER SEVEN

The shuttlecraft lifted smoothly off and out of the freighter's hanger bay. Joel had punched in the coordinates and now let the craft and its computer approach the earth size moon. The moon orbited a large hot planet about 100 million miles from its medium sized orange sun. The scans gave it a time frame that indicted the sun was in its last throes of existence before collapsing in about ten thousand earth years. The moon imaged signs of water but inadequate for colonization. Most of the water was in just one place, and it churned and seethed with some veracity. Scans showed that the explorers would have to suit up with protective covering to shield them from the heat. Joel had planned to land at one of the poles where the temperatures were not so severe.

The craft made one revolution to interpret any unusual formations or anomalies, but found none. Pocked marked and barren in most land areas, Joel had the crew buckle in as he eased the craft down to what looked like a flat, temperate surface. With the slightest of trembling, the shuttlecraft came to rest on the service as gently as a mother's pat on a baby's backside. With years of experience, Joel was pleased, as was his crew as they applauded his achievement. They each began to document readings about the outside environment before Joel would allow them to suit up.

Rod and Midge were fairly drooling at the mouth to get outside.

"My scans report that the temperature is only about 50 degrees Celsius, but the atmosphere has only ten percent oxygen, not enough to support us for but for a short time. 80 percent nitrogen but it is mixed with methane and some rare gases. So I suggest full hazard gear." Joel gave his report in a formal like voice. The suiting up sounded like wisps of space cloth against the new nalon fabric.

The others all agreed about going outside and it was only minutes before the group was suited up, except Dirk who was ordered to stay aboard for a variety of reasons. Joel wanted someone to stay behind for any mother ship messages. Dirk had admitted that in his profession he had little experience with this type of research or knowledge with space suits. This was enough for Joel to have Dirk stay behind. The others gently cajoled Dirk for his hesitancy to venture forth on new ground. Dirk's long aquiline nose and large glasses nodded in a muted acceptance.

An excited group entered the decompression chamber and cautiously exited to the moon's surface. The only indication of this moon's existence was a notation on one of the space charts as moon TQM 621. An indication of third quadrant moon 621 in the area.

Midge had fallen to her knees, fully engrossed with rocks and debris covering the moon. One could see it was her passion. Rod had lifted his electric binoculars, and he was scanning the immediate area for any signs of disturbance or habitation. No chance of any real revelations but it was his job and profession. Slowly the crew moved to the south to a safe distance to try again for any new information about this part of the moon, when suddenly the warning buzzer on the shuttle sounded as well as a radio transmission from Dirk came to the attention of Joel. The copilot smartly answered the freighter's summons.

"Joel Kerr here as commander of the shuttle Sprite."

The voice on the other end was Sparks with a message of great interest.

"We have received an answer to our earlier transmission to base. They are mad as all get out and ordered us to return with the girl post haste. Whisper's father sent the message himself. Make a few quick observations and then return to the ship. Captain wants all to return to the ship, as we are to shove off upon your arrival. Cap wants to keep our several weeks distance as an advantage until we find a better place to stand aside MacPherson's arch and let the old war horse's posse pass us by. Ten four."

Joel signed off as he motioned his little group to return to the shuttle. They had taken a few samples and some pics for analysis. All complied as the ship was being readied by Dirk for trip back to Hope Merchant. When all inside, they began to chatter about the turn of advents as well as their appraisal of a quick survey of the moon TQM 621.

"Not enough time to give an appraisal of its composition," said Midge in her small squeaky voice. Her plump face was pink with exertion and unreserved effort. She replaced her tools, and kit with a polished and smooth manner.

"No dud here," thought Joel as he watched with the eye of an eagle.

The trip back was quick and uneventful, just as Joel had wished. He piloted the little craft into the freighter's ample hanger bay with only a final caressing hiss of the ship's on board hydraulic systems.

A message was waiting for Joel to come to the pilothouse immediately after he had debriefed and freshened up. No doubt, Rusty wanted a confab about the newest developments. When Joel had completed his necessary tasks, he went to the pilothouse as ordered.

Captain Bolt was with wife, Evie. They were both engrossed over some galactic space charts.

Joel broke the intense silence with, "this sure looks like a wonderful way for newlyweds to meld their minds and souls. If I didn't know better, it would appear that you two are planning some nefarious space activity."

Rusty looked up with that queer toothy grin of his as he put his arm around his friend. Looking straight into Joel's eyes, he spoke with a somewhat seriousness Joel was not accustomed to hear from his old buddy.

"We've got trouble, real trouble, right here in river city, old buddy. That old warhorse used several expletives in his return message that had our punishment written throughout it. My plan is to move out again in hyperspace on the ARCH and keep our two-week advantage alive as long as we can. His Comet Chasers will be speedier, but even so, it will take them a few days to find our exact plasma signature and a few more to get within scanner range. I figure in five days we had better find a place to hunker down and allow the chasing parties to pass us by. We can then determine their tack and reconfigure our line of travel on the ARCH to miss any meetings of Battle and his boys. If we hurry, every hour counts in our favor. Have you questioned any members, trying to locate any counterfeits?"

"The only one that I have observed and found to be the real genuine article is Midge. She just poured herself into the geology métier like a dog after a bone. Rod also seemed to fulfill his appointed profession. I had Dirk stay on board the shuttle to monitor the craft's systems while the rest of us ventured onto the moon's surface. Nothing to relate that could be called exciting, I guess. "

"Well, we have exciting fish to fry as Battle Winslet sets out to overtake us before we reach our destination. Have Whisper come up here so I can ask her one more question of great interest to me."

Lieutenant Commander Kerr made his way to the cabin section of the ship. He could sense more than feel Rusty setting the controls for a jump into hyperspace. A duty they usually fulfilled together. This event underscored the urgency that the captain felt about leaving the sub lights speed condition and return to hyperspeed on MacPherson's Arch. The small cabin of Whisper's was not occupied so Joel decided to try the recreational area. That Area was also void of the little lively Miss Winslet. Next, Joel entered the Library but no Miss Winslet, only Dirk Dare reading so intently that he didn't know of another's presence until Joel politely coughed.

"I am just catching up on some scientific material that might be needed as we finally get to our destination."

The studious Dare was almost quivering in his reply to Joel's sudden appearance. Dirk looked as a boy caught looking through a play man magazine. He quickly closed his reference magazine and dutifully asked whether he could be of any help to Joel.

"I am Just trying to find whisper for the captain and thought she might be here in the library."

"I haven't seen her of late but would suppose she has been helping Midge with care of the animals in the rear of the ship."

Joel thanked the studious fellow and returned to the corridor that led to the aft section of the freighter. It was a long walk, but Joel was careful as he forged ahead to be wary of all the machinery and crates that could still hide a malcontent that wanted to rain confusion or havoc down on the mission. The passageway was not well lit and provided many creaks and squeaks of unknown origin. Finally reaching the aft section where the animals were, Joel could hear Midge and Whisper's conversation. He didn't mean to eavesdrop, but the words came to him as he approached.

Midge's very feminine but high-pitched voice of the nasal variety was speaking. "He doesn't know or care about it."

"Hello there," was Joel's greeting as he entered the area.

"Mind if I interrupt your duties for a minute?"

"No, of course, not," was Whisper's terse reply. She added that they were almost finished with the animals and wanted to know what Joel wanted.

"The captain wanted to see you, Whisper. As we are starting to hop into hyperspace, I would suggest you go to the pilothouse right a way. I can help Midge with any last minute animal chores so you can leave immediately."

"OK," was all she said as she turned on her heels and left the area?

The captain was fussing with the controls when Whisper arrived and announced her presence. Her demeanor was relaxed and causal as though she belonged here in the pilothouse. Her salutation was close to flippant but had overtones of camaraderie.

"Whatcha you doing boss?"

Being gregarious was one of her more endearing attributes, thought the captain. Her presence on the ship could pose new problems for all, thought Rusty, as the whimsical girl stood before the captain at a mock attention. He would have to make a lot of changes in the duties as well as dispersing of supplies including the availability of stasis sleep chambers if he decided to use them. She must know her father holds the key to our success, thought the harried captain.

'Can you tell me Miss Winslet if your father will be taking your mother on a trip of this nature?"

Whisper appeared to be taken back for only a split second as she relaxed her stance. Her piercing blue eyes focused on the captain as she framed her answer carefully and skillfully. Her mouth formed a tightly compressed line of pretentiousness. She was slow and almost coy as the words fell from her lips.

"Why do you want to know? What difference will it make? Why do you think I would know? Radio him and ask yourself, captain"

Why are you so defensive Miss Winslet? I just wanted to have the information in my head for any possibilities of leniency on the part of your father in case this mission comes to a bellicose action."

"Well, if she comes she will have some sway over the old war bird, but if she doesn't your goose is cooked. She rarely comes on his regular forays but this time it may be different because of the possibility of colonization."

"Whisper, when we get to the planet in one piece what would your plans be in the colony? No available men to seek out for marriage. Only loneliness and boredom."

"Let me worry about that as I have been lonely all my life with an over bearing father and a rustic as well as domestic mother with few chances of outside relationships. My passion really is for teaching and learning. I love to read, and I write poetry profusely. Does that answer your questions?"

"Yes, Miss Winslet it does. You may return to whatever you were doing when my summons interrupted your activities."

With seriousness on her face Rusty had not seen before, the girl smartly turned and exited the area.

Rusty really found out very little about Mrs. Winslet's possible accompaniment of Battle on this chase mission but he did find out a lot about Miss Whisper Winslet. "A very polished female," thought the captain as he finished his calculations for jumping into hyperspace. The captain with the final lift of the red safety latch protecting the jump button, punched it with the conviction they were all going to complete this mission safely and successfully.

Rusty Bolt

CHAPTER EIGHT

Battle Winslet was furious. An underling had not replied to a very specific transmission and tried to garble any answer. His mind was on fire with all kinds of visions of reprisals. Red faced and full of guile he began to make calls and commanded action on the part of base functionaries to accommodate his requests. The entire base knew of his ruthlessness and responded with a velocity not seen in many a day. Dispatching his wife to his quarters, he informed her of the severity of the situation. 'Lost daughter' and all that. Blenda was to accompany him on this mission 'for the families sake.' Bring my kit and caboodle that is packed in the back room and pack your self for a long voyage.

The ships he had partially commissioned were ordered to make haste in their preparations for lift off. He would have to finalize all regulations and requirements after take off,' he thought.

The base was all a twitter with the suddenness of Battle Winslet's preparations for a few standard test flights, they were told.

Within only hours, the two Comet Chasers had been fueled with extra fuel and readied for the Counselor's send off. A test that was testing the bases' proficiency? They seemed to be over loaded with supplies and exploration equipment. His wife and son were seen at the staging area, a puzzlement to the base officials. A young man from the academia's brightest academic ranks was also at the staging area. Lambert Bright was considered the man with more knowledge about space and space ships than anyone alive. He was only in his early twenties but had graduated magma cum laude and other honors before he was sixteen. He had gone on and excelled in all of his endeavors to the point of embarrassment of his peers. He attained Captaincy at eighteen. This was an accomplishment unheard of at the space academy. Lambert is a good-looking lad with bright eyes and an intelligent forehead that complimented a mass of straw colored hair. A tall man with square shoulders and a penchant for controlled emotions. The entire Winslet compliment of family friends and some dignitaries began boarding the two Comet Chasers with solemn efficiency. Some in Battle's craft and some in Lambert Bright's craft/. A task much practiced?

The company was soon nestled in accommodations for a long ride to where? Battle made light of the hurried preparations. Each Chaser was full at a compliment of twelve persons each. Some married and some not. Some well versed in space travel and some not. Some professional geniuses and some not. It was what Battle had chosen as cronies, friends, experts, and family. He would have to soon explain to everyone all of the mission's goals as well as the rations needed to continue the flight for a long period of time with little special accommodations for lengthy missions. They all trusted Battle Winslet completely. Battle piloted Chaser One and the young space prodigy Lambert, piloted Chaser Two. Captain Lambert Bright was enjoying all of the excitement as he proficiency logged in all of the coordinates with a speed that defied description. Soon, the small crafts were launched with sub light-speed into space without a jolt or buck. "Lambert Bright must be at the helm," came a few murmurs.

As the hours passed, a few passengers became discomforted and found a commander to complain to. When advised of the possible yearlong journey, the comments and activity became rancorous.

The commotion rose to mutinous proportions. Battle on his ship went up and down the aisles appeasing each and every captive to this journey. Some expecting this explanation and some not.

When on autopilot, Lambert who had been advised of these conditions earlier, went to each passenger with the revelation of a long and cramped voyage. The reactions varied quite a lot. Some acted very pleased to be included in a venture of this kind and others quite irate that full disclosure was not forthcoming earlier. Mrs. Winslet on Battle's vessel gave out the cabin assignments. Blenda Winslet was very capable at placating her charges with her smiles and tested marital relationship. Blenda was a lady of average but compact proportions with an uncanny ability to see more than what showed. She was a handsome woman with a contagious countenance. Fiery azure eyes that could bore through you, accompanied by salt and pepper hair that spoke of maturity, wisdom and trials. Her teeth were straight and white and made her smiles radiant. Battle was certainly blessed with a wife of these affable dimensions.

After awhile the clamor died down to a low snore that permitted the business of explanations and directives to be issued to one and all. Passengers began to depart to assigned cabins and allow their disgruntled feelings a time for correction. Battle and Blenda, spent time going over the amounts of provisions and oxygen supplies. With recovery equipment on board as well as ration packs, they could easily make the trip if no anomalies appeared. Their only real concern was the passengers' temperaments and boredom. Very little recreational equipment was on board a Comet Chaser. 'Cards and puzzles and vision screens would have their limits,' thought Blenda. She would have to take over being the social director as well as keeping Battle from doing anything regrettable, on this voyage. She knew it concerned her daughter and the clandestine way this mission was orchestrated. That truth gave her a few more gray hairs at her early age of forty something. Not the best of situations for a past Miss America, some years ago in her previous single life.

Some hours later when all was quiet Waver discovered a slight malfunctioning with one of the two engines on Chaser Two. It would have to be repaired before it burned out like a lightening bug's ardor in the morning. Informing his father of the engine's discrepancy, Waver was rewarded by Battles pernicious observations.

"This will require a full stop out of hyperspeed and removal from MacPherson's arch. It must be done," said Battle with bitterness in his voice, when Waver informed his father of Lambert's informed need for this delay. "I'll keep Lambert on course so he can make the eventual rendezvous with those miscreants in the Hope Merchant, if I can't, roared Battle, as the words rang with rancor

Waver, clumsily took to the radio and transmitted to Lambert the orders of his father. Battle kept interrupting his son with other directives to be transmitted to Lambert. After a painful time of interruptions and revisions, Waver and Lambert terminated the transmission.

With deep sighs, Battle pulled out of hyperspace and hyperspeed to be berthed in space like a fly on flypaper near MacPherson's Arch. With great heaves of discontent, Battle called on one of his passengers who were supposed to be fluent in space ionic plasma engines. The man was well versed in the engines and indicated a speedy repair. Carl had descended to the engines but had to wait while they cooled off. Carl asked for some special tools for the job. Waver was diligent to get them from the maintenance bay offering to help as he returned. Carl was non-committal for the time being while ascertaining the exact cause of the malfunction and trying to determine if Waver's expertise existed in this matter. When the engine cooled, Carl was bothered by constant inquiries by Battle as to the extent of the engine's malfunction and how long will its repair take. This irritated Carl no end, consequently he took his time making evaluations and adjustments. Waver didn't help much by pointing out meaningless things. The failure found was too complicated for Carl to explain to Waver or his father. What he needed now was a part that regulated the plasma burners. The ship didn't have a spare one Carl was told. That will mean I will have to disassemble the regulator, find it's flaw and attempt to repair it. A time-consuming application of talents utilizing the most excruciating exactness.

Battle was infuriated with the news but held onto his wits when he finally offered if anything he could do would expedite the operation.

"Not really. I have to have a competent assistant to help me with the delicate procedures."

Waver looked at Carl with a painful expression. 'His meager talents were not needed here,' he thought as venom was rising in his throat.

"I'll just go back to the helm and see if I can flummox anybody there," said Waver to himself in a caustic arrogance way.

"You go find Walter, the man in cabin two and send him back down here to help Carl with this repair. Then see if your mother needs your help in any way," said Battle to his son.

Finding Walter and relaying his Father's command, Waver lazily drifted towards the galley. The son moved to the middle section and found his mother attempting to prepare some food for the passengers. The various stores were in a haphazard manner, making it difficult to find what was needed. The haste of departure was no doubt the reason. This part of the trip was planned to have regular fare and prepared by a chef or some comparable person. Blenda nominated herself and was having great fun as Waver approached with hanging head. "Can I help?"

"Certainly, just wash you hands and find some condiments for the people. Place them on the table. Your father is going to have to notify his groupies, that each person is to have a job or a productive function for the balance of the trip. Two or three people cannot do everything."

By and by, Waver found Walter in cabin two sending him down to Carl. Waver passed his father at the control room, trying to see if he made any mistake in the message concerning the engine malfunctioning. He heard his father confirm that all the readings had confirmed the engine's malfunctioning. This gave Waver some of his confidence back as he returned to the mid-ship sector, looking for the condiments his mother had asked for.

Waver was in those awkward teenage years that always presented new and mystifying conditions on a daily basis. He wasn't stupid, just a bit clumsy in finding the right thing to do in his elder's eyes. He liked working with his mother for she was so forgiving and pliable.

He was glad he had not revealed to the engineers where he thought a spare regulator for the plasma burner was errantly stowed by him. Thinking of his faux pas, he spilled the tray of condiments on the floor, fomenting coos of forgiveness from his mother.

RUSTY BOLT

CHAPTER NINE

The days passed quickly for the crew of the Hope Merchant. Whisper famously managed to be gregarious with everyone with the possible exception of Gloria, who felt as though Whisper had eyes for Joel. A false assumption.

The story began after about two months on MacPherson's arch. Scans and calculations were made practically every hour with no serious observations or deviations of the planned flight. A chore not absolutely necessary but prudent. Joel worked the scanning equipment in a small cubical beside the radio shack. A responsibility he shared with Sparks. The chair there was always empty so Joel would just plop down and begin his scanning operations. This one time when he entered the little cubical, Whisper had earlier seated herself in his chair. Joel when seeing this just treated the scene in a frivolous or boyish manner and sat on the lap of the young Miss Winslet. Unfortunately, at that very moment, Gloria was passing in the corridor outside the cubical. With her fists set on her hips, Gloria stood in the doorway, eyes on fire, viewing the awkward scene.

"Well now, how long has this been going on?"

Joel, immediately stood up and motioned Whisper to vacate the seat and cubical. As Whisper passed close by the indignant Gloria, the green monster of jealousy shot arrows into the heart and head of Gloria.

As Whisper exited, Joel began to explain the situation to Gloria. With precise words and truthful declarations, the young copilot made an acceptable, convincing case for himself. A bruised young wife ultimately refused the entire dialogue.

"Joel, I saw what I saw and I am not amused or flattered with this type of conduct. You may call it a youthful prank, but I saw things in that girl's eyes that didn't belong there. Your big grin didn't help any. Just continue to notice that our sleeping arrangements will have to be altered until I have enough time and evidence to think this thing through to a final conclusion."

After Joel had related this lamentable information to Rusty, Captain Bolt made the decision that some were going to have to go into the sleep stasis units for a period of rest. A time for the body and mind to recover. A time for errant synapses to correct their alignment.

After a week of relative normal operations, Rusty and Joel put their heads together to determine the number and candidates for the sleep procedure. After weighing the facts, and some wrangling the two leaders suggested five names that they thought would agree without any discord. The five were notified and the results presented to them as though it were an order. The two leaders were fully aware that if one or two dissented with the order they had no way of forcing anyone to obey. The five sleep units had been ready for some time, but the consensus had been to wait for a more advantageous moment to actually utilize them. Now was the time Captain Bolt told his group of five notified crewmembers?

In attendance were Joel, Gloria, Whisper, Midge, and Rod Wheeler. The reasons were not discussed although the group was in a mild state of quandary. The most common comment was," Why me?"

The captain explained that this procedure was used by all of the deep space commanders to renew the crew's metabolism and psyche powers. Captain assured them that no particular reasons were used in selecting the five members present.

Captain Bolt revised his slightly prevaricating statement with, "that it was the captain's prerogative to select members at his discretion." This seemed to mollify the group of five. The murmurs soon died down as someone asked, "What's next?"

"Dr.Walther and I will accompany you to the sleep area tomorrow at 10 A.m. Then we will fit each member with the mantles and fit the medical paraphernalia to permit the stasis to begin. The timing will be set and all will regain consciousness in two months where upon the next five will probably enter the same situation as you are in now."

At 10 A.M., the next day the group assembled at the appointed sector. The preparations and procedures went smoothly even as Whisper and Gloria traded barbed glances. Gloria had dark circles under her eyes and a definite down turning of the mouth, adding years to her previous youthful appearance. Joel also had lost his humor and showed definite signs of lack of sleep and concentration. Whisper seemed to be little affected, as her comely smiles and wholesome countenance were still in place. Whether it was real or some type of theatrical performance, Rusty wondered.

All the procedures went smoothly, and it was only an hour or so before five bodies and minds had entered a state of tranquility and important rest.

Dr. Walther exclaimed she had some difficulty with two of the sleepers. "Both Joel and Gloria's bodies seemed to be under much stress and agitation. Could it be the little misunderstanding they had a week ago?"

"It appears so. That was one of the reasons I started the sleep process now. It will give the five a chance of renewal of all their faculties. You know doctor, we will probably have to be in the next five unless events change my mind."

The doctor looked away as she left the chamber with the comment thrown over her shoulder.

"I guess no one is indispensable."

Taking one last look at the five and their chambers, Rusty didn't want to leave this part of his crew indefensible and unable to give advice.

With a heavy sigh, of leadership Rusty left after glancing at all the dials and gauges that monitored the sleep process. All of these notations could be read at the pilothouse also. Should he lock the compartment for safety? "Yes!" He made the entrance to the compartment a locked portal. Thinking of the possibility of a saboteur on board, the key and code numbers stayed with Rusty for safekeeping.

Captain Bolt returned to the living quarters and requested a meeting of the remaining crew by using the ship's intercom. All remaining members converged at the pilothouse as requested and waited eagerly for the Captain to give reports, orders, and any recent news.

Not a single question was uttered. Most, if not all the crew were aware of the tiff between Joel and Gloria and, the part Whisper had played.

"We have completed the stasis process for five of our crew members. We must all be very diligent to perform double duty where and when needed. This new tasking will be for two months. The scans will continue, and any news will be reported immediately to me. We will have some drills as usual to prepare for any contingencies that might arise. Our faith and hope are in the hands of God, but we must be dutiful to exercise our responsibilities perfectly. I am giving temporarily, the duties of copilot to Dr.Rexanne Wheeler, as her skill as doctor will be on an 'as needed basis.' This will allow her to be free for her to be next in command. I will appoint added duties to each crewmember in a separate manner, later. Any questions?"

"Captain, what of any news about the possible Comet Chaser that we were told about several weeks ago?"

"After much discussion and statistics we concluded that anyone following us on MacPherson's' Arch, even at hyperspeed, could not advance any faster than the speed we are going. Therefore, we have concluded that the Comet Chasers could not catch up with us. With that thought in mind, we have decided not to worry about them but have maintained constant scanning for safeties sake. Any other questions?"

No one offered any other questions, so the captain dismissed the little group, so they could return to duty.

The Captain wrote in the logbook of the events of the day. Usually, he could bounce off of Joel any thoughts that could be more accurate or graphic than Rusty had observed. Rusty called Eve to come to the pilothouse for a minute of two. Eve left her culinary skills in the ample galley and went forward as the captain had requested. When she arrived at the pilothouse, her husband met her. He was exhibiting some stress in his facial features. "What's up, my captain," was her salutation?

Captain Bolt looked up with admiration and observable relief. His face had a gray pallor when she entered, but it soon turned healthy pink upon Eve's arrival. It was like magic. He was smitten by this lovely lass.

"Eve, I miss Joel something awful already. He is a very valuable asset to me, and to all of us. We have done so many things together I feel as though my commanding right hand has been removed. I know Dr. Wheeler will perform as copilot admirably, but I want you to keep an eye on all that is happening around us so we do not have another misunderstanding of the harmful kind. Keep an eye on me also so that none of my actions could be misinterpreted or deleterious to the mission."

Eve responded in her special feminine way. "Certainly I will. And you can count on me keeping an eye or two on you at all times."

About that time, Dr.Rexanne Wheeler entered the pilothouse and ensconced herself in the seat just vacated by Eve Bolt. The two newly weds exchanged pleasantries with the doctor, and Evie returned to her assigned task.

"Well captain here I am here to learn all I can about co-piloting the freighter. I had only some basic training about flight procedures, but you can teach away for I am a fast study for about anything. Did my resume help in this assignment?"

"Yes it did. It helped me make this choice, and I am convinced it is a good decision."

The two were soon deep in flight jargon as Rusty showed Rexanne all the necessary maneuvers for flying the Hope Merchant. Rexanne was a fast study and it showed as she learned all the names as well as the control's functions as the call for chow by Evie.

The new abbreviated crew met for a lunchtime meal prepared by the loving efforts of Mrs. Bolt. It was at this time Sparks was given permission to divulge the results of his latest scan.

'I have made the scans as deep and as wide as possible without concentrating in one direction, which gives us a very wide-range look at the space around us. This is in all directions. It gave nothing out of the ordinary. With this type of extended scan, one does not have the ability to interpret the findings with clarity available on closer or narrower scans. Finally, I concentrated the scan in a narrow band at our rear for a short time. This far-reaching narrow scan was evaluated by Captain Bolt and me earlier, indicating we have some type of object following us. It appears to pulsate. We are not sure if it is a celestial body or a terrestrial body. It can hardly be the Comet Chasers, but we will have to be on high alert for if we can detect them they can detect us. The distance relates to over two or more months before any encounter of the calumnious kind happening."

All eyes fell on Captain Rusty. Their forks were frozen in midair like garden statuary as he commented.

"Not to worry. It is probably an asteroid with a short life, randomly following our ionic signature or our energized cosmic dust. Maybe a coincidence or an unusual anomaly. Our next scan will likely show no presence of a body or mass that is on the same course as we are on. Eat up and be happy."

Rusty was encouraged by his own words but the knot in his stomach was still tied.

RUSTY BOLT

CHAPTER TEN

Lambert Bright was not accustomed to be in complete command of a star vessel like this Comet Chaser, but he quickly found his place as a fair and competent flying officer. The vessels were of a military class, different than the earth's transport boats and galactic cruisers

His straw-like hair was now close to his forehead as the perspiration of responsibility made it so. His copilot was a much older man of cautious, hesitant responses to the young man's orders. The entire ship was still in a state of mild disbelief, and confusion, concerning the yearlong journey. Some had an inkling of its length and duration. Some had been on long voyagers before and had prepared mind and body for this eventuality. Some just stared in mild agitation and apprehension. It was with this group that young Mr. Bright was asking about each of their skill levels and past professional backgrounds.

Old Battle Winslet had told him what his objective was on this mission. "Follow Russell Bolton and the Hope merchant on MacPherson's Arch and make him return to base after turning over Whisper Winslet, his daughter."

Lambert had a very certain conviction that once the pursued had jumped to hyperspeed, the Comet Chasers had no chance of overtaking the Hope Merchant. His vessel, the Comet Chaser Two was fast but had no chance of overtaking the freighter if it stayed in hyperionicplasma speed. Battle must have known that also but in his exuberance he thought Lambert could somehow make a difference. Lambert thought long and hard, trying to figure out a way to modify his ship, knowing they would have to stop to make any modifications, only causing further delays.

Lambert hit upon an idea of his making that would not require a leaving of hyperspeed. It was along shot but in Lambert's mind a possibility. He found in his enquiries that a man was on board with extensive knowledge concerning transportation of molecules and ions. His name was Garner Trapp, the very man with special experience Lambert needed.

Lambert left the pilot house in charge of Co-pilot Bristle Fume; Lambert and Garner passed down to a lower deck and in the forward section found the apparatus that Lambert was seeking. Lambert had disclosed his plan to Garner who in turn thought it to be feasible. This part of the ship was a complicated array of electronic computers, diodes, and telegraphic cells. Lambert and Garner were soon taking wires, cells, diodes, ionic phasers, pulse adapters and making new connections, disconnecting old relays, modifying armatures, amplifying plasma relays, until their certainty of success was sorely tested. The area was close as was the air sparse as each of the two men finally in exhaustive unison uttered, "I'm finished."

The hours had passed quickly as Lambert returned to his pilot's seat. The ship had been on autopilot as Lambert found his copilot nodding off in a fog of boredom. Bristle Fume was noted for his penchant to sleep whenever the occasion presented itself.

Lambert in mock sonorous sternness spoke, "anything of interest happen while I was gone?"

The barely older military man came to an abrupt wakefulness and postured with a faint salute.

"Not a thing out of the ordinary except the dials and gauges were occasionally jumping and changing occasionally, like something was messing with the drive motors. They soon settled down."

'An indication of the two men working in the lower forward compartment,' thought Lambert. It was now time to test the two men's electrical manipulations. Lambert found the toggle switches and buttons needed to fulfill his concept of a projected motion in three dimensions with molecular appearances. The idea was to scan straight along MacPherson's arch with a projection that would appear to be a body moving along the Arch. The gathering of scanning arrays in a concentrated single projection would increase the scanning signature and distance ten fold. This would deceive any pursued vessel with rear scanning abilities to mistake the image for a gaining body on the arch. Lambert pushed all the buttons and switches for activation. The ship's lights dimmed as a low hum was being emitted throughout the ship. It was a success, but it could only be activated in intervals as the setup strained the vessel's electrical systems and her batteries and generators. This would cause the Hope Merchant Vessel to erroneously detect a body following its ionic signature.

This was a good a step in the right direction but Lambert knew that the pursued would have to make a faulty decision and come out of hyperspeed to descend the Arch and attempt to hide as the pursuer passed on by in hyperspeed. A good scanning technician could detect this maneuver and come out of hyperspeed to apprehend the pursuing ship. This scenario was the only one Lambert could imagine catching the unheeding freighter, Hope Merchant.

The electrical ruse was flashed on and off for the next few months. Lambert had no way of knowing whether the gimmick was working until they could scan a vessel coming off the arch. A feat of extensive proportions. Lambert kept several of his worthies busy constantly viewing the forward scanning screen for any variances that could indicate any of their target's imperceptible movement. Lambert was still uncertain what he would do if they did catch the freighter. Battle indicated earlier Lambert was to only retrieve his daughter. How could he accomplish this without the assistance of Father Winslet?

The ship's roster was becoming more complacent because of their comparative closeness and it being imperative to survive. With only two sleep units for stasis, it was a real challenge to keep everyone happy and mentally fit. One of his passengers was a medical doctor to help in the sleep chambers. Most of the assemblage eventually called Lambert just plain Bert. It was easier and much less formal for all.

Bert assured everyone that he was doing all he could to reestablish contact with Battle Winslet as well as maintaining the pursuing of the freighter, Hope Merchant. Most of the passengers had been given some small assignment to keep everyone busy. This plan was working well. The ladies took charge of social life aboard the craft, cleaning duties, food preparations, and the like. While the men helped with maintenance and labor requiring essentials, crates and parcels of all kinds had to be cataloged and assigned new areas for balance or sequential order. It was a harmoniously occupied group but would it last a year?

Battle Winslet and his helper, Walter, tirelessly worked to repair one of the plasma regulators. Waver tried to help but was waved off by his father. The task of fixing the crashed regulator took more time than Battle had contemplated. The exercise caused him to accept in part defeat.

He put all his trust in Bert Bright's ability to catch the Hope Merchant with his daughter intact and tried to be nonchalant to others about the whole business. Nevertheless, inside he was seething with the rage of a wounded bull. His wife tried to placate Battle and give him a sense of worth with words of encouragement.

"We possibly will still have an entire planet to colonize with your expertise and direction. The message we relieved said that Whisper was unharmed and happy. That has taken a load off of my mind. Our joy should be in that truth as well as the adventures ahead with or without any punitive repercussions handed Russell Bolton and his crew."

Battle received her words with specious affirmation. He loved his wife but knew she had no grasp of command or worldly matters.

"My dear I am aware that all things will work out by my will power and prestigious abilities. We all must bide our time, and energies that will eventually prove my plans and purposes are correct. This will be more evident when we arrive at our destination. Even though it is months away I will not lose my intentions as time will actually accentuate them."

Leaving the captain's quarters, Battle returned to the pilothouse. Battle and Walter had repaired the faulty regulator and were in the process of calibrating all of the ships propulsion capabilities. It took time doing it right. Battle, estimating they had lost about five days repairing the damaged part, a partial galaxy in distance, eventually gave the command to go to light speed and then to hyperspeed as

Walter held his breath and crossed his fingers. Walter lifted his red cover switch and ignited the engines for lightspeed. The Comet Chaser two gave a hum with an accompaniment of whirling noises, indicating the ships advancement to lightspeed. At this very critical moment, Battle lifted his red cover and switched the toggle to hyperspeed. The ship responded as he had expected with all regulators working smoothly and harmoniously. Star lines disappeared as the ship moved onto MacPherson's Arch, attaining a speed at many times the speed of light.

Battle had explained the phenomena to one of his underlings (Walter) only a few days before.

"The science behind hyperspeed and molecular transference with computer thought manipulations . We start with plasma ionic resonators. First, we achieve lightspeed, by activating the plasma ionic regulators and at that speed, we launch out by magnetic particle intensifiers. This gives us and obtains the second light speed, now going twice the speed of light using resonators with rhythmic pulsators. This process continues a several thousand times in a microsecond. One speed being launched forward upon the last. Computer thought waves that out distances any light speed attains this movement. This velocity coupled with the discovery of MacPherson's Arch permits us to travel in space at a very rapid pace. The center of this travel is the gathering of molecules around the resonating molecular transference resonators in a definite space, of our Comet Chaser, and contents. A phenomenon that permits the gathered matter to travel not only at extreme speeds but allows the matter to pass through other matter. This is accomplished due to the form of matter, having space between all molecules, allowing under these circumstances to pass through without collisions, molecules of matter in a relative static position. This also permits the moving molecules to pass through so fast no heat of resistance is generated. It is the only way to travel in the vastness of space with asteroids, stars, solar systems, and Comets that one might run into. No communications are possible in this state. The discovery of MacPherson's Arch was by sheer accident on one reconnaissance mission by Evans MacPherson. He found that the Arch on the fringe of the universe bent the time and space continuum so that distance could be attained outside normal perimeters. All in all a leap forward for mankind."

Walter had absorbed most of the teaching and nodded with the eye of comprehension on all counts, dutifully giving Battle a warm feeling for his effort. With this warm feeling, Battle now became completely immersed in the complexities of the flying of Comet Chaser One. His chase now included Chaser Two after the freighter that imprisoned his only daughter. All on board Comet Chaser Two hoped in silence that their captain would not stumble or err by his rambunctious nature.

CHAPTER ELEVEN

The Hope Merchant continued to show its worthiness by flying in hyperspace at hyperspeed flawlessly. The ionic scan continued to reveal something behind them on MacPherson's Arch, but it only fluctuated, never gaining any distance. Captain Rusty Bolt made a decision that was bold but necessary. They would no longer concentrate on a narrow rear scan but would revert to normal wide scans. This conclusion was based on some objects pulsating naturally with no apparent advancement. Wide scans would be more prudent and revealing of space matter of interest all around them.

The two months went very quickly, and the five sleepers were awakened punctually to the relief and joy of everyone. Each participant awoke with refreshed faces and eager anticipation of renewing duties and responsibilities. Joel was so happy he appeared giddy. Gloria also radiated a new vitality and countenance. Whisper alone projected her same radiant self, but with renewed strength and purpose.

The crew gathered for one of Eve's famous gourmet dinners complete with gentle spirits. There was much lighthearted conversation by everyone. It dealt mostly with the renewed feelings of anticipation and a sense of well-being.

Joel tried to get Rusty to commit names to the next group to enter the sleep chambers without any immediate success. Actually, it was obvious. Only six remained to enter stasis.

"You will love it, cap. I feel as though I could work and concentrate for days without any additional rest." A boast of unnecessary proportions because Rusty had in the past availed himself to the sleep stasis condition. Its benefits were most amazing.

The crew also wanted to know who would be the next five to enter the sleep condition. There were five volunteers so they would be next.

Whisper broke the camaraderie by speaking.

"I suppose I could go back in because of being such a bad girl."

This comment terminated the dinner's fellowship. Immediately, Rusty was aware that a reconciliation between Gloria and Whisper had to happen. Harmony was going to be achieved to make them one big happy family once more or more sleeps might be needed. Rusty wanted to conclude this subliminal agitation between the two ladies before escalation or contagion occurred. A rubbed surface turned into a blister. With those things in mind, the captain quietly requested the two women to remain behind as the group was exiting the dining area.

"I would like a word with you Whisper also you Gloria. The two young women obeyed the biding of their captain and ensconced themselves on opposite sides of the table.

"You must know ladies how important a smooth running, happy ship is to the success of this unique mission.

I can have no ill feelings on board. The mission cannot afford any discordant feelings of passions. Jealousy is not to be manifested in any manner on my ship. I want you to shake hands as you forgive each other of any menacing feelings you may have of any kind. Come on now and forgive and shake, it won't hurt a bit."

Slowly but surely, each lady moved toward the other to shake hands while mumbling words of sorrow and forgiveness. The actions resulted in each moving around the table to hug and cry their way into friendship's golden realm. It took only minutes but had everlasting positive results.

"You may return to your cabins and subsequent duties."

An order carried out with unusual dispatch.

"Now I can effectively command this ship with the harmony so much needed on such a long and arduous journey," spoke the captain as he hoped for his copilot's eventual return. After all, several months of rest would give anyone a lot of catching up to do.

A week went by with the smoothness captain's only dreamed of. All hands were in a heightened state of anticipation as the time was rolling by. "Are we there yet," became a constant salute for everyone.

After a time of retraining and drills, the group was conditioned to permit five more hands to enter stasis eagerly. Rusty designated Eryka, Sparks, Eve, Rexanne, and Dirk to enter the sleep chambers. There was no fussing or dissension as each realized Captain Bolt must stay awake and command his ship at this juncture. The months would roll by and still have time for Rusty to sleep before locating the planet in question. The sleep procedures went smoothly as Dr. Wheeler had instructed Gloria in the art of blood transference and inert gas fusion. The temperatures began to lower as all gauges and dials registered normalcy. The entire procedure took about an hour and was accomplished flawlessly by Gloria and Rusty in attendance. Rusty again was the last one out of the chamber viewing all indicators and locking the area. He would miss his Evie very much.

The days and months rolled by with no difficulties in maintaining all of the ships operations. The scans revealed nothing new or noteworthy. The engines and computers performed impeccably. When the prescribed months passed, the captain unlocked the stasis chamber to find that all systems had functioned perfectly as indicated by the gauges in the cockpit. The five-crew members were brought back to a state of normalcy without a hitch. With hugs and congratulations, the crew soon returned to weeks of rhythm and proficiency. The only area of complaining had been the lack of superb culinary artistry. This was of course, was due to the absence of one Evelyn Bolt. Gloria and Whisper in tandem did their best to furnish and prepare food to everyone's liking, but it was just not the same. No complaining came forth because all were aware of the effort being exerted by these two women, so recently in disharmony but now the epitome of compatibility.

The cruise took on an air of a recreation holiday as the chores became more and more routine. All hands were proficient when the drills were called even at unexpected times. Eventually, Rusty got in his sleep requirement with Joel in command with nary a difficulty.

Rusty and Joel had talked about the artificial gravity that the ship provided and had determined to land on a planet or moon with the same gravitational force of earth. The crew needed the full force of gravity to tone their muscles and other organs. This procedure should have been done earlier but with an unknown behind them on the arch, it had been delayed. The ship's ability to duplicates earth's pull was minimal at best so the long journey required a few stops to acclimate one's self to the body's requisite optimal function. The moon stop gave little such advantage.

Sparks made hourly scans to find such a place as needed. After about a week of scans, a planet was located in a solar system much like earths. They would come out of hyperspace and hyperspeed to land on this rock. First, the planet would have to be orbited to locate an advantageous place to land. All of the environmental projections would have to better than any planet they had scanned recently. One of the reasons for this long and arduous journey was that no planet had ever been found to incorporate all of the environmental necessities of earth to sustain life as known by mankind. Some planets came close, but for long durations of time, none had been found that radiated all of the qualities of the blue planet. This scanned planet ahead had poles that were temperate. Oxygen ratios were suitable for humans. The only detectable defect was a mist of vapors that contained some sulfur and trace amounts of inert gases that might hinder normal breathing. The crew could wear masks and tanks of purified air if to the surface when feasible.

The freighter was alive with activity when they heard the news. Each hand gathered backpacks of air and camping equipment as well as personal items for a seven-day stay. Only Rexanne seemed a bit apprehensive and when questioned by Rusty her reply was simple.

"I hate to leave my surgery and books and go outside with no desire for exploration of this kind. I came to be a medical force on a new and agreeable planet. I have always been uneasy with camping and all that. I am aware of the needed benefits this trek will have for everyone. Therefore, I am in agreement to go but will have a hard time being happy." Rusty thought that was a good and candid answer and joined the others at the portal of exit. They traveled once around the planet, and Joel had seen to it that the ship was out of hyperspace and hyperspeed. Coming off of MacPherson's Arch was a delicate maneuver that Joel and Rusty had practiced in simulators many times on earth. This time it was just as smooth with Joel making all of the correct calculations. The planet showed a gravitational pull of 1.1 and would be sufficient for their needs. Rusty would be first out of the decompression chamber. The door made the customary hiss and opened to a strange planet with grasses and rocky debris everywhere. The mist was wet and smelled of eggs. The atmosphere for the adventuresome was tolerable if accustomed to a few mature eggs in the wind. Most of the crewmembers carefully removed their breathing masks and walked about slowly as it was some time before gravity would have its therapeutic effect. With weak knees and with demanding bodily effort, the group sought out some high ground to establish a camp.

The mist seemed to undulate. It would rise and almost disappear and then descend with regularity. The intervals were about an hour in duration. When it fell the only side affect was one of odor and diminished distance for observations.

The crew made the most of their situation. Sleeping in late in their snug sleeping bags, having campfires at night as well as some forays into the areas round about gave them some variety to temper the journey. These treks had found that they had camped by an adjacent area filled with bubbling mud pots. Thermal vents added to the area's odor, which the campers were becoming accustomed to. All of this helped the planet to have a temperate area. Not too hot and not too cold

It was a lazy kind of week for all when at the end of the seven days, someone came down with a medical emergency.

Midge Dare had been out in the fields gathering samples for analysis had developed a slight cough, accompanied by a slight fever and abdominal cramping.

Because at first the symptoms were minor, the group finished packing up and returned to the ship in a normal manner. Midge was sent to bed in the infirmary with constant monitoring by Rexanne and Evie. It was shortly confirmed that Midge had appendicitis. Rexanne found that there was muscle guarding at McBurney's Point. The classical symptoms increased to the point that Dr. Wheeler announced an operation must be perform immediately before any bursting or perforation occurred.

Midge and Dirk became concerned because of the shipboard's untried operating room. Dr. Wheeler assured them that is was an easy and common procedure she had performed many times.

"The surgery area is up-to-date and completely stocked with everything needed for the procedure. You won't endure any lasting pain and will be up walking around tomorrow with only minimal discomfort."

Midge and Dirk were relieved by Dr. Wheeler's comments. Even Rod Wheeler gave a big smile at his wife's confidence and abilities. Rexanne had asked for volunteers with some medical experience to help her. Whisper was the first to offer her services and added that she had worked in nursing homes as an aid.

It was all settled for the operation to begin by asking all non-participants to vacate the area that was done post haste as Rusty marshaled them into the corridor.

Whisper and Rexanne had donned white operation gowns, masks, and gloves. A scene that Midge could do without. Soon, Midge was asleep with some kind of new anesthetic that was pleasant to the nose. The two women began the procedure with Rexanne calling out the surgical requirements and Whisper fulfilling each one with surprising adeptness. In a very short time, a small incision was made in the abdomen where bleeders were sutured off and more muscle cut in a precise manner. Because of the plumpness of the patient, a little more time was needed before the minuscule offending appendage was located. The operation was completed and the patient was recovering as expected.

Dr. Wheeler was hesitant to report all of her medical findings except to the captain and Midge when she was up and around. The finding was both good and unexpected. Rexanne sought out the captain on day three of Midge's recuperation. The patient was recovering nicely as had been expected. But, when Rexanne revealed to the captain that Midge was doing satisfactorily as well as being a mother in about seven and a half months, it took Rusty by surprise.

"It's only just and proper that you inform our little ensign geologist of her condition if she didn't already know. Let's make it a joyous occasion even though it might curtail her geological explorations for a time. We must expect things of this nature occurring even with all the options available to prevent pregnancies."

Rexanne went immediately to find Midge to give her the news. She was found in the library poring over some reference books. When the good doctor told Midge of her condition, Midge was nonplussed but relieved.

"I wasn't sure but I had all the symptoms but wasn't certain until now. Dirk will be so pleased because of his shy and reserved nature; he had surmised we wouldn't be able to have a family. I will go and tell him right away."

Midge left the library while Dr. Wheeler pondered about the numerous elusive complications that would ensue with an infant on a new and unknown planet. The Doctor could hear the celebration that was happening down the passageway and felt regret that she had not told the whole story.

Rusty Bolt

CHAPTER TWELVE

Finally, Rusty reluctantly agreed to enter sleep stasis, after avoiding and utilizing the chamber. Two more volunteered just for the sheer pleasure it provided as well as the relative passing of time. Whisper and Midge had been having trouble sleeping without sleep aids so it just might be the thing to do. At the last minute, two more volunteers made their requests known to the captain. Dirk and Eryka had similar reasons to enter the sleep chambers. Eryka had complained of some bronchial distress since the planet of mud pots and was certain a sleep stasis would help her return to robust health. Dirk just mentioned he would be lost without Midge. The five assembled at 10 A.M. as prearranged, looking like penguins lined up for a dip in the pool. Rexanne and Joel made all the required adjustments and maneuvers to complete the procedure. The others had left after their "good byes" and "see you in the spring," comments.

Rexanne waited until alone with Joel and related her findings. "Joel, I have to tell you about some of Midge's medical results. I didn't tell Rusty because he was so in need of the rest. I am telling you to get it off my mind and hope you will relay this confidential information to Captain Bolt when he returns from stasis. My testing on her when the appendectomy was performed showed early signs of leukemia that could endanger her life as well as her baby's. I hope that the tests will eventually show a false positive. I will do more tests when she has had a chance to rest, and I would have had a chance to study in detail about tests for confirmation. She seems to be in remission now. I would think she had some inkling of this and it would have shown up on her earlier exhaustive medical examinations. I think the sleep stasis does her much good somehow. That and a usual course of action on this ancient sickness is the best I can do. I am at a loss to recommend to you on a course of action now."

Co-captain Kerr replied that a wait and see attitude was what he would recommend now. This just added to the burden of his while the captain was taking a much-needed snooze. An irate father in pursuit, and a sick patient of great importance to the mission, a dog without his kind, and a possible saboteur still unknown. One of the good things about this voyage thought Joel was the perfect <u>operation</u> of all the complicated equipment.

Only a few days later did Joel Kerr recall his earlier words of praise. No amusing retorts on this level, he thought.

The craft had given the slightest sign of trouble by infinitesimal pulsating quivers. Joel was almost unwilling to give Sparks the order for a complete diagnostic of all the ship's functions. A lengthy, time consuming, and energy draining difficult procedure may reveal more than Joel wanted at this time.

Holding his breath Joel had Sparks begin the diagnostic assignment.

Sparks Walther didn't even ask why? The tone in Joel's voice gave the required encouragement to get on with it without questions. While Sparks was busy with the complicated programs, Joel went to find Gloria for a confidential conversation. Unloading his burdens onto Gloria, she was quick to reply. Gloria was not shy about giving advice so she did.

"Just be very sure you tell no one until you tell Rusty when it is possible. He will deal with it as a captain must, even the pulsating quivers you sense might not be serious. The news about Midge's medical problem will prove to be a false positive, especially as she comes out of stasis. Maybe by then Rexanne would have found some new test or even an experimental treatment. Maybe the tests are actually inconclusive. I noticed earlier she was deep in study in her own medical library. Honey, it's going to be all right, I just know it."

Joel had maintained a personal diary as did Rusty. Above and beyond the ship's log, it contained Joel's own personal thoughts. This day he wrote:

Just got news of another wrinkle in our mission. I have been told by Dr. Rexanne Wheeler of the recent diagnosis of one Midge Wheeler. She reported that she suspected said crewmember had leukemia. Captain Bolt who is in sleep stasis does not know this new revelation. Dr. Wheeler has been seen studying her medical books for any recently discovered way to defeat this insidious almost ancient malady. My course of action will be to disclose this information to Captain Bolt immediately after he returns to normalcy and wakefulness. I am now having Sparks run a complete diagnostic of all the ship's functions. I felt that this was necessary because of a slight abnormality in the rhythm or pulse of the engines. I will go and help in this task and hope to report later of any negative findings.

Returning to the electronics area, Joel found Sparks hard at work. The man was so engrossed in his work he did not notice the copilots presence. Sparks Walther was a big man with a wide forehead, now covered with sweat. He was talking to his displays before him. It was a study in seriousness and assiduity.

"Come on hydraulic pressure! Get up there and be happy! Ok. Gaseous fusion resonators do your complex stuff! I don't want any of you try to go past normal! Now this is good. Make me happy! You all are trying very hard, and I am going to be relieved. Pretty ladies touch on normal to make me smile."

Joel felt it would unwise to disturb the big man so he just removed himself from the area quietly. He would come back later.

Joel went to the pilothouse where Eve was monitoring the banks of gauges and indicators. They were all on autopilot, but Eve just wanted to be certain that her husband's ship was functioning on all levels efficiently. It was an exercise of extravagant devotion towards the Captain and the mission. When she noticed Joel, Evie immediately went into an excitable dialog.

"We are getting very close to our destination. The scans are showing we are approaching an area of black holes. The ship's dials and indicators may go into a phase of erroneous reporting. Being so close to the goal of this mission I have formulated a hypothesis about the inability for anyone finding our planet on scans or any other detection devices, such as deep probes. The light coming off our new planet has been pulled into a black hole making it invisible to scans and probes."

Having gotten Joel's undivided attention, the chef par excellence continued with a seriousness that was unusual for her character.

"If this is true, I am troubled that MacPherson's arch comes too close to one of these black holes and may pull us into its gaping orifice. This apparent reality has the ability of ending our mission and us with it."

Joel was hard pressed for an answer that would quell Eve's uneasiness, but he tried.

"I am sure that Rusty will have a plan of action long before we enter such a dangerous place. He has an uncanny ability to circumvent all kinds of difficult situations. I have seen him in action when all others imagined doom and despair. He dug deep into his repertoire of knowledge and beat the odds. He will do the same this time, I am sure."

Eve was assured by her friend's comments but said she would like to remain here. "Staying and monitoring the ship's computers gives me something to do and makes the time fly."

"I think that's a good idea. I will be glad to relieve you occasionally if you so desire."

Joel left the area with the assurance that Eve would keep an eye on all of the gauges and computer indicators until her husband was again on the bridge and in command. Joel would relieve her when necessary.

The sleep commencements came rapidly. The coming-out celebration was just as exuberant as the ones before. Most of the crew managed to squeeze in the cramped stasis quarters. Congratulations, all around as the sleepers began to orient their thoughts as they also shot rapid-fire questions.

"What has been happening?" "Are we there yet?"

"Any news about our pursuers?"

"I am starved. How about our feast later?"

"How close are we to our destination?"

One by one, the stay behind crewmembers answered the questions. Rusty and Eve were reunited and retired to the captain's quarters but not with out 'a good job' directed at Joel for his time as commander. Joel parted the couple by saying; "I have some interesting news that I would like to convey to you when you are ready. I'll be at the bridge." It was only a normal time later that Rusty joined his co-captain in the pilothouse. All shaved and showered, looking as though he was going to officiate at a ballroom dance.

"How splendid we look my captain," said Joel with a twinkle in his eyes. "I see your time was well spent, as reunions always are." Rusty replied in a good-natured way.

"Just get on with your report, my funny joker."

"Dr. Wheeler informed me that when she performed the appendectomy on Midge, she took a lot of additional tests. Some of these tests gave an early indication that Midge was in remission with a form of leukemia. She is also pregnant with a child that might not make it as well. Rexanne has been busy studying her medical books for any ways to beat this thing. I haven't told anyone and was waiting for your assessment for a resolution to this problem. In addition, the gages and indicators have given us a new worry. I detected a slight; quiver in one our hyperdrive engines. I am having Sparks run a host of diagnostic scans as we speak."

Rusty ran his hand over his face in a typical fashion to wipe away all of the negative news he now must face. His was his manner to take a few moments and ponder the ramifications of these kinds of events. Joel knew that to be the case, and he waited patiently until his captain was ready to verbalize his conclusions. Joel had also mentioned that the area had some very threatening black holes that have shown up unexpectedly. All in all the captain was weighted down with problems not of his own choosing. He would try to solve them one by one.

CHAPTER THIRTEEN

Captain Bolt decided to call Rexanne and Midge into his quarters to discuss the medical ramifications of the leukemia problem. He thought it best to get all the facts out into the open so that it would become clarified of rumors and erroneous information. He summoned them to come now, so that he could tackle the problem of errant engines and intimidating black holes later. The two ladies arrived together with serious faces. He had them sit down as he wondered if his wife should be present. Rusty excused himself as he summoned Evie to sit in on the confab. When all were settled in, the captain offered a few pleasantries and then got down to the subject matter he wanted resolved.

"Ladies, it came to my attention of a medical situation that needs to be divulged and discussed candidly. If the good doctor will explain about Midge's condition further at this time, I would be most grateful."

Dr. Wheeler was ready with her answers as she began to tell about the tests and her exhaustive research on the subject. Midge was taken back but heard her discourse with a certain confidence in her friend. The doctor continued.

"I would like to make further complex tests so that I can rule out any false positives that might be hiding in this scenario."

Midge asked, "is there any immediate danger to my baby?"

"I don't think so at this time. You are young and now well rested so that all the further testing hopefully will give excellent and more accurate results. If you have more questions, I will be glad to discuss them in my surgery with you, if that is acceptable with Captain Bolt."

Rusty gave a quick and favorable answer. The meeting was over as all participants left the captain's quarters to attend to other matters. Rusty headed for the electronic shack and his good friend, Big Sparks Walther, who was still tinkering with all his evaluating gadgets of vast importance on a mission such as this. Sparks was tapping gauges and indicators while making the air blue with his comments. The captains words didn't startle him as he gave a big sigh as he turned to meet Rusty's gaze and inquisitive countenance.

"Captain, I have looked at these results and indications for two days and I still can't get my facts straight. I was hoping you could give a gander and decipher some of this gobbledygook."

"What seems to be the crux of the problem Sparks?"

"The gauges just seem to jump around and will not give a consistent reading. When I go to make a printout of the findings, the results are different from only seconds before. The engines are also giving odd readings so that no adjustments should be attempted. My gut feeling is to continue with all the same paradigms we had originally assigned and pray for the best. Now is no the time to abandoned MacPherson's Arch."

"Good advice. It is must be our closeness to the black hole in this quadrant. I would like to observe the instrument panels for a little while so that you can take a break and I can determine if any other course of action might be taken. If you see Joel please send him up here."

The big electrical wizard remained for a while in case of explanations. Rusty busied himself by fiddling with dials, gauges, computers, and relays effecting no real change. The engines were making only slight deviations in their rhythms, and the black hole threat still seemed far away. The summation in his mind was that the pull of some more immediate force was disturbing the instruments. Maybe it was a black hole forming and not yet powerful enough to give an identifiable signature. Sometimes in their formation, they give off a signature of minimal importance. Much like a distant star cluster. Sometimes no indications at all. With these thoughts in mind, he turned to matters that are more enjoyable. A repast with his close friend and wife would be in order after such a long morning of decisions and challenges.

Captain Bolt gave Sparks Walther a comment or two about his tenacity at the control and scanning panels. Sparks replied that he would return to the electronics after contacting Joel. Rusty thought to himself how fortunate he was to have such a friendly and dedicated crew.

Leaving the wheelhouse after Joel came, Rusty retired to the galley where savory aromas filled his senses. It was this warm feeling as he began to eat the sumptuous meal prepared by Evie and Gloria. Joel soon joined them.

The few weeks remaining flew by as each day, new challenges and difficulties arose to be effectively dealt with. The computers and gauges settled down, giving expected and accurate indicators. As a crew of over-comers, this should be a group most ideal to colonize a new planet. All the members were asking which day they would quit hyperdrive and depart hyperspace and MacPherson's Arch. Rusty and Joel as well as Sparks studied all the configurations and came to a decision to approach the planet in sub light speed and that would happen in about 3 days. The crew wanted a celebration. The ladies all supplied the cooking skills needed for such an occasion.

Whisper had become one of the crew as she quit asking about scans to the rear indicating a possible pursuer. Her questions were answered the same. "No sightings of any kind that would indicate a pursuing vessel." This satisfied the young lady resulting in a more placid individual. She wanted to make a desert that she had perfected on several tries during the year. It was her famous dump cake that everyone raved about. Made with canned peaches, similarly to her grandmother used to make, she said.

All except Joel, who was left in charge of the ships controls and scans, attended the mini celebration. Joel came later. All of the computations had been worked out and entered into the ship's computers for activation in just under sixty hours. A watchful eye was still needed, stated the Captain, so Joel volunteered. They had endured much on this flight, and it was with great relief that all of the members entered into games and singing as well as enjoying a meal that would have been suitable for royalty. Food supplies remained adequate according to the chefs. As the group was milling about, Rusty surreptitiously viewed each member with an eye towards any inconsistency.

Evie and Gloria were to be trusted completely. Their loyalty had been tested numerous times. Their background checks were flawless.

Dirk Dare and his wife Midge presented a complex picture. Dirk was a man of gentle intelligence. A man with ears that had no ear lobes, just disappearing into his jaw line.

Nose of aquiline proportions with large round eyeglasses making Dirk looking much like an owl. He had proved himself often in a reserved type of way. His joy level was never very high, however; Midge was usually bubbly in a plump type of way compensating for any the couple lacked. Midge should have known better than to start out on a yearlong mission without practicing some type of method to prevent her pregnancy. Why was it not used? Why were her recent medical examinations unable to detect any signs of her leukemia? Surely nothing sinister here. She has been a rock of intelligence concerning all other situations.

Rexanne Wheeler was a fine doctor with great humanitarian incentives. Her ability to rise to the occasion was noted frequently proving her loyalty and practicing her profession.

Rod Wheeler was harder to dissect. He was a big man with his famous bushy mustache that quivered when emotional. He appeared to love his work but showed cautious affection towards his wife. He didn't seem intimidated by his wife's high status as a doctor. No information from them on how long they had been married. Their resumes stated nine years. Hard to figure.

Eryka was positively a beauty and had eyes only for her husband, Sparks. She excelled in her ability to act, as she had performed several nights of plays she had written and then directed. Everybody just loved her for her varied abilities. She was very good at her climatology duties that were revealed on several occasions.

Sparks was positively the best electronics expert Rusty had ever worked with. What he didn't know he found out immediately by books or experimentation. Rusty was inclined to believe that everyone was who they said they were and went on and enjoyed the festivities before relieving Joel so he could enjoy some of the remaining evening. Rusty relieved Joel, to the copilot's exuberant exclamations of bliss. "It's all yours, boss, everything is normal and even the engines are now purring along like caressed kittens. How is everybody in the recreation room? Any fall down comical antics yet?"

"I was just thinking about all of the crew, and I am more convinced of their genuineness now than any time on the trip. We are blessed with a group that is full of energy and knowledge, and it is up to us to see that all of that is put to good use in the weeks and years ahead. Many difficulties lay ahead, but these folks will take them on one at a time and overcome," said Rusty with a sigh of relief.

"Ever one is sober as a newly elected Judge," Joel said as he hurried away with another comment over his shoulder,

"Keep a sharp eye on for any for black holes. You know how they can fool the scan's interpretations. I don't want my supper interrupted."

Rusty was left alone with all of the humming and clicking of instruments of information and power. He settled back into the bucket seat for the intense observations required at this important juncture of the mission. One erroneous calculation or untimely activation could spell doom to the entire yearlong mission. With these thoughts in his mind, he picked up the readouts that Joel had captured. They all spelled normalcy. That was what puzzled Rusty as he put into his personal computer the numbers so that it could crunch them anew. To his surprise and horror, the numbers did not match.

Rusty with great haste summoned both Joel and Sparks to the bridge. When they arrived, Rusty was quick to reveal the discrepancies and sought their explanations and remedies. Each man exhibited a slack jaw and eyes of surprise. Joel was gulping down some hurried foodstuff. The bridge took on a rare quietness as their minds began to discern the troubling news. Sparks was the first to offer any type of tidings.

"Captain, I have been reading these instruments for about a year and have noticed no major faults in any of the reports or indicators. Maybe we should check all of our results for any minute variances. How about your personal computer? Could it some how be at fault in reading minor fluctuation when there is none?"

"My computer has been tested by me several times with no variances. The ship's computer is off by only a billionth of one percent. Not much for usual work but can be fatal when we must need absolute accuracy over quad trillions of light-years. This reconfiguration must have taken place back on earth to make us abort the mission or land light years away from our destination, thereby giving someone else the advantage of first discovery of the planet New Hope. Let's also use Joel's personal computer for varification,"said Rusty.

Joel could only blink his eyes in disbelief as he realized he had relied on the ship's computer for an accuracy that was almost infinite. He cleared his throat and offered up this comment. "I can get my computer to examine the equations again. If yours is correct, we have hours of reconfiguration ahead of us. With only three days for corrections, we may be cutting it too close. I am willing to work night and day to save our bacon."

The group agreed to try Joel's personal computer as well starting on the new codes needed by the ship's computer to register correctly all of its diagnostics. When Joel's computer read the ships data, it also noted the minute error on distance and speed. Evidently is was not the black hole distributing strange instrument behaviors but it was the ships computer trying to correct itself when entering in an area of recent scan readings. This was going to take a Herculean effort by three very intense men.Much time in the ship's library lay ahead.

RUSTY BOLT

CHAPTER FOURTEEN

Rusty Bolt left the bridge and informing his two helpers that he would inspect some of the electrical conduits for any signs of tampering.

"I won't be gone long, but I have a feeling that the tampering may be internal or at least it might have been done at the base by someone that had access to the ship and adjusted the computer's codes by tapping into the computer cables in the conduits. I want to see what type of tampering job that the saboteur has done."

"Hurry back," said Joel and Sparks in unison with some anxiety showing in their voices.

The captain, with his cap pulled down tight on his head moved to one of several conduits that housed electrical cables and air ducts. The computer cables were housed in one of the smaller conduits and Rusty was aware of the tight fit he would experience when following the cables. Reaching the entrance to the ductwork, he released the front panel that permitted access. Looking at the opening Rusty wondered if this job might be handled better by someone smaller, like Eve.

She wouldn't know exactly what to look for. Rusty had explored theses ducts several times, before leaving the earth base and would have a good idea of what to look for. If any disturbances were spotted, Rusty could try to determine what type of tampering transpired. Was it an amateur or a specialist? A specialist might indicate a job executed on earth. An amateur might indicate the tampering happened while the ship was in flight.

Inching along the narrow and confining duct, Rusty began to experience a feeling of frustration. The mission was no threat to anyone if successful. The motive must be one of jealousy or maybe even a mental imbalance. Killing all of the Hope Merchant's crew would not be known except by a few. Even old Battle Winslet would not find any comfort in the destruction of this mission. He knows his daughter in on board. However, now when he thought of it, the old warhorse could not contact Hope Merchant. The ship could not contact him as well. When the repairs of the logs and codes of the ship's computer were made and the necessary correct adjustments entered, Rusty knew the ship will have to come out of hyperspace so that it will be able to attempt to contact Battle's ship, if it is still on MacPherson's Arch. Since Battle was following us, his ship would have also been on flawed vectors to disaster.

With these thoughts rolling around Rusty's brain, he had finally moved to a place that showed where the intrusion of false information occurred. It was an amateur Job. The break in the cable was rough and still exposed. The culprit didn't have all of the necessary tools to leave the cut in a neat appearance.

Taking some electrical tape that he had brought with him, the captain wrapped the cable and wire to give the break the required insulation it needed for perfect transmission. A few wires were also correctly repaired. Moving very slowly in a reverse movement Captain Bolt was able to extricate himself from this confining place. On the way out, he noticed and retrieved a small piece of cloth that had been torn as someone had been in a similar position as Rusty Bolt. It was very small and of the denim kind. A fabric that almost everyone on board wore at one time or another. Placing the piece in his teeth, the captain was soon free from the duct and returned to the bridge immediately.

His two crewmen had worked out numerous codes and file changes, just waiting for the Captain's authorization. Captain Bolt quizzed them on all points and asked for double checks and verification of all changes by using the back up computer's files and programs.

"Boss, if we punch in these numbers in the next three hours, all of the corrections will permit us to land on New Hope in less than two days off our original projections, but in a different position."

"I feel confident in your computations, men. I have repaired the cables so that the ship will get back on corrected parameters. As your Captain I give you permission to punch in all of your corrected codes and numbers while praying for perfect success."

The corrected discs and chips were inserted into the main computer without so much as a whimper or blink. The big on-board computer was reading and digesting the corrected numbers just as it was supposed to do. The three men looked on with awe as each realized that all of their lives as well as this life-giving mission were now in the hands of diodes, chips, and nanafers. The computer when finished gently corrected the ship without noticeably being changed. The momentum and velocity of the big freighter changed as well as more accurately adhering to the wide upper band of

MacPherson's Arch, giving greater accuracy to that position. When all of the work was finished, the men noticed it had taken only twelve hours to fix, most probably because of the amateurish abortive alterations. An expert would have made changes that might not have been corrected. With a sigh of relief, the three satisfied men returned to the recreation room to see whether anything of interest was happening.

To Rusty's relief there was nothing exciting happening in the rec. room, so he found his way to his quarters after giving Joel and Sparks his sincere thanks and many words of appreciation. *That is what a good captain should do on a mission such as this*, thought Rusty. Joel was given the task to return to the pilothouse to monitor the ship's progress at this delicate portion of the flight. Rusty would return later.

Since the ship was in competent hands, Rusty went to his quarters there to find Evie engrossed in another book. Evelyn had read almost all of the books in the library. They were of an entertaining nature as well as some reference books that interested her. She also had a few cookbooks scattered over her desk. Delights yet to come?

Rusty entered with a scowl on his face that Eve noticed immediately. He was thinking about the patch of fabric he had found in the ship's ductwork. He would pose some questions to his bright and intelligent wife.

"What is troubling you hon?"

"I found a scrap of cloth in the duct work that contains all of the main computer's cables. It is just a small piece of denim I found near the place where an amateur had spliced into the computers cable to interrupt codes and numbers that would have put us off our destination and caused us to crash or continue on infinitum. The change was very minute but at our speed and our computerized molecular positional alignment, it would have caused disastrous results. I was wondering if you had noticed any one of the crew with a

100

tear in their jeans that this little piece of cloth could have originated from?"

"All of us wear jeans made of denim. Most of the females wear them tight; in fact, Whisper makes them so tight there is no room for anyone to not notice or comment about any tear in her jeans. I think that if any one of us noticed a tear in our jeans we would discard them or at least never wear them again. No need to ask around, I suppose, because who would admit such a thing that happened under suspicious conditions?"

Rusty was considering Evie's comments when he made an unusual request.

"Could you check the waste units in case some pieces may still be showing? Also, if you can tactfully find out if anyone noticed, even if subliminally remembers, or could identify anyone having torn jeans."

Evie, smiled and gave her husband a nod and wink as she replied, "I can get the information if it is possible. When I put my mind to it, I feel I could get water out of a pile of sand."

With that bit of boasting, Evie turned and with sleuthing movements, complete with an imaginary magnifying glass, moved out in the passage way and disappeared from Rusty's appreciating gaze.

Captain Rusty Bolt left his quarters as he fingered the scrap of cloth in his pocket. Rusty could not believe anyone on board could be responsible for the computer tampering. In his mind, he pondered over each crewmember and their character to reassess his position about them. Arriving at the bridge, he continued his mental gymnastics. "Maybe it was not a crew member but someone at the earth base that had to work in a hurry. If we all died or just failed in this mission who would benefit. Only Battle Winslet would try to sabotage this journey before he knew about his missing daughter," mumbled the Captain

The thought process began to produce a tightening around Rusty's forehead. That created a migraine that was not needed or would be tolerated. The final resolution had to be a complete trust in his crew. No other conclusion would be tolerated because of the need for absolute dependency when tasks were delegated to each member.

Joel was in attendance, but asked to be dismissed as he said he wanted to take some time off and get up to speed on his diary and biology studies. This left the copilots chair empty so it was very natural that when Whisper entered the pilothouse she sat down in that seat. The bucket seat completely enveloped the girl so it looked like an inflated embrace of a leathery grandma. Whisper's face looked more serious than her young years should support.

"I wanted to come forward and tell you about my father and his visions of grandeur. I know he had information about this mission even before you did. He had seen the unmanned probe that came back to indicate an unusual but similar condition on earth. He had wanted to orchestrate a mission to the area, but you beat him to it. That made him mad as he had planned to rescue some of his cronies and intelligent friends before earth became nearly uninhabitable. He requisitioned some Comet Chasers and had them hastily retrofitted for long distant missions. At that point, he saw you were ahead of his project and had to formulate a crafty plot to delay or stop your progress. He could have ordered you to cease but that would cause too many questions and inquiries to delay the missions. What he devised was a scheme to alter your computer by only a minute change in codes and files. He enlisted me to do the job, ergo my having a special pass. I refused to go through with the plan so he enlisted some indebted lackey to do the job. Ignoring my father's command was the reason for me to hide aboard your vessel. I tried to find the place where the alteration had taken place but when I found it, I realized that I was not proficient enough to make the changes back to original settings. I wanted to tell you, but I remembered that the changes made by some one of my father's employ would be infinitesimal so that harm or hurt was probably going to be averted. I almost forgot about the alteration but just now when talking to Evie I noticed she was giving my jeans a very scrutiny. That must have been when I tore my jeans. No doubt, she saw the torn pair of jeans I had disposed of earlier. I hope that you will forgive me because I have come to like all of the crew and wish for this mission to be a resounding success. I also believe my father has somehow found a way to follow us with his bunch of people that are toadies to his whims." Whisper was trying to restrain tears that stung her eyes when they finally came forth.

"Now, now, Whisper I appreciate your confession but we have now rectified all computer alterations and will experience no problems in our goal or landing. I wish you had come forward sooner. We would have had more time to make all of the corrections needed. Incidentally, I had Sparks beam a concentrated scan to our rear and found no hits that gave us any concern. If your father is still following us, they have made no perceptible gains. We will need every one's presence once we make our landing; in fact, we are preparing to make many preparations for that event right now. You can be a real help to anyone of the crew that might require assistance in their profession's landing requirements. It might be to everyone's advantage if you not mention your confession at this time."

Whisper vacated the copilot's seat with a sigh of relief. A heavy burden lifted from young feminine shoulders. Rusty did wonder whether he was told the truth, the whole truth and nothing but the truth. The little lady had to balance her love for her parent with the safety of the Hope Merchant.

RUSTY BOLT

CHAPTER FIFTEEN

The ship became a hive of activity. The excitement approached delirium. One year in flight was a record at super-mega hyper speed. Traveling over billions of light years made it possible only by MacPherson'Arch. All crewmembers were preparing for the landing that was fast approaching. All that needed to be done was to come out of mega hyper speed and leave hyperspace and MacPherson's Arch as planned and programmed into the main computer. Rusty watched the controls for the exact instant to leave MacPherson's Arch that would dissipate at the same rate as the ship's degrading of speed and velocity. Joel was also in attendance as the numbers were called out on the execution of returning to sub light speed so all of the planets features could be seen and monitored. Joel's clear but controlled voice was heard. 10,9,8,7,6,5,4,3,2,1 punch! The big freighter hunched its mammoth structure for only a split second as star lines disappeared, and a solar system of recognizable familiar features appeared. A medium size sun of a yellow-orange color that was millions of miles away, displayed its grandeur. Several smaller planets orbited the sun with a blue planet, like earth, in the desired orbit beyond the glare or intense heat of the yellow-orange orb. This planet was so situated that it was behind other planets, so probing scans from earth never fully recognized its potential for colonization.

Captain Bolt moved the spacecraft closer, and everyone could distinguish planet features. New Hope was the name given automatically without any planning by the crewmembers. It fit the scenario as Hope Merchant banked for a nearly perfect view.

The shapes of water and landmasses were varied and in no way resembled, anything they had seen on this trip. The atmosphere appeared blue white with masses of moisture floating near the surface. The water was of a blue-green nature that suggested oceans. The only deviation to a regular sphere was its infinitesimal bulging at its equator with water in that area of an elongated outline. The planet appeared to have bulged in its creation by throwing part of its matter out to an edge as it revolved. The equator was the bulge. Minuscule but detectable. It was not so great as to alter its revolutions or its slight polar inclination. The scans were working busily to transmit all relevant information to the craft, thereby permitting Captain Bolt to make an informed decision as to where to land his vessel.

A land mass was noted that gave the appearance of a temperate zone as well as having abundant vegetation.

"Those might be trees," Joel ejaculated as his Captain pointed out the area. Low murmurs were heard by Rusty as he began the actual descent that would require all to eventually fasten themselves in seats with safety belts.

"Its beautiful"

"It will be great to put my feet on terra firma"

This evoked a little laughter. (No terra here)

"I can't wait to start a garden"

Rusty knew that was the voice of Evie.

"Won't it be great to start everything from scratch?"

That was probably Whisper's comment.

Sparks was heard to say, "I wonder if radio transmissions can be made in this atmosphere?"

Midge muttered, "Look at all that area to investigate."

Even the dog, Pep was excited and gave the assemblage a few barks of anticipation.

"OK. Ladies and gentlemen please take your seats and buckle up for the landing of this auspicious journey. We will have to go around the planet at least once more to effect a satisfactory deceleration before landing. Just sit back and enjoy the views," Rusty said with excitement in his voice also.

Eventually, the big ship made for a patch of land that was nearly surrounded by water and had hills and dales to afford protection from any inclement weather, for all the instruments indicated earth-like climate conditions. Seeking the perfect spot of firm land and finding it, the freighter touched down with nary a thump. All on board gave themselves and the captain a vigorous round of applause as well as many sighs of relief. The captain began to read the environmental readouts that gave every indication of livable conditions, including temperatures and oxygen levels. The Captain gave Joel the order to advance to the pressure chamber for the orderly exiting of all members. The only caution was to exit one at a time based Joel's assessments. This all went very smoothly as each member exited and then took in great gulps of fresh air into lungs desirous of the real thing and not recycled air.

Pep managed to exit with Whisper even though his first choice had been to be first one out. The captain opened the storage bays for easy access, so that all of the pioneer apparatus could be removed for immediate use on land. Folks were carrying living units, cooking utensils, bedding and even the land crawler was extracted for trials and travels. It was difficult to maintain any order. The group was very excited to settle after a year in a confined space. Even with this excitement, the Captain had warned of the possibility of a short stay because of unknown variables. This was to be an exploratory location only. It was still an orderly pandemonium but with a kind of sweet communal orientation.

Dr. Wheeler and Rod were beginning to erect a portable first aid station. The hubbub was contagious as captain and crew alike worked together to prepare for the weeks of exploration and pioneering ahead. All thought of any pursuers was no longer on any one's mind. A dangerous condition as the crew would find out.

The land crawler was unpacked and readied for exploring. Rusty and a few others took off on a scouting mission, to find out the lay of the land. Pep was running along side of the crawler and disappeared into the brush from time to time to the barks of discovery and happiness. Even as Whisper's continual attempts to keep the dog by her side became futile.

Captain Bolt, Rod Wheeler, and Eryka Walther with Whisper in the back, all set out in a southerly direction via the crawler with weapons and protective clothing. They were going to the top of the highest hill for an advantageous viewing position. The trek became difficult as the humidity and sun soon made the trio uncomfortable warm but not deterred. The highest hill was quite a way off from the landing and when the group finally reached the top, they were amazed at what they saw. In all directions the land mass was dotted with small ponds of water with very thick vegetation all around little ponds. The other unusual feature was that the trees and vegetation appeared to be in an orderly arrangement, almost as though they had been planted that way.

Rusty placed his elecnoculars to his eyes for a more intense scrutiny of the landscape. He could not see any sign of life except the vegetation that suggested a fertile soil and an abundance of moisture.

Pep came up to the crawler a tired but very happy canine. In his mouth was a small bone that was inspected by Rusty.

"Well, something is alive on this planet of an animal nature. Pep has proven himself a great hunter and now we must be great gatherers. Eryka, I want you to make some sketches of the lay of the land. Rod, if you would find any unusual land material to take back to Midge, I would appreciate it. I am going to take Whisper and Pep on a tour of this hill top for possible discoveries only a sensitive dog nose can tell us."

The little group left the crawler to expedite their Captain's orders. Eryka moved to large rock that gave her a better view of the unique landscape, checking out wind, humidity, and air pressure.

Rod was scouring the top of the hill looking for any animal life or soil that gave an unusual report from his small electronic scanner. No beeps or a burp yet, was in his mind as he came across a shiny specimen that was surely unique to him. The geologist, Midge, collected other pieces of the surface for study.

Rusty, Whisper and Pep who was now on a tether were moving through brush and trees at a rapid pace. At least for the canine.

"There must be critters here, Pep. If you can smell them I can eventually see them," muttered the Captain.

The dog was relentless as he found small animal trails and tried to follow them with breakneck speed.

"Whoa, little doggie! We have found all I want to find this first day. Let's just take our time and make forays another day."

The dog seemed to sense that Rusty had run out of steam and obeyed the commands to stop and return to the crawler but with some canine hesitancy. The three explorers found Eryka and Rod already at the vehicle with enough results to take back to camp.

"What did you folks and Pep find, Cap?"

"Nothing much of interest except small animal trails and a few deserted burrows that Pep declared uninteresting."

"What did you find your scavenger hunt?"

"A few shiny pebbles and some sand as well as I collected some special vegetable matter, maybe Joel would be interested in."

Rusty looked at the sketches Eryka had made and congratulated her on her talent for detail and completeness. The little group sat awhile and just looked at the scenery while Pep tried to doze because of the boredom.

Returning as conquering heroes, they were beset by both welcomes and questions. The material that Rod collected was given to Midge, to her joy of working again in her field. Joel with thanks to Rod, received the vegetation, for thinking of him. Rod's big mustache worked overtime in grateful appreciation of the comments from his friend . The camp had taken on a look of homeyness as the live-in tents were placed in a circle. The doctor's medical tent was situated at the center of the circle, a place where Whisper and Pep would be housed. The cook's tent was behind the ring with a pathway in the loop to facilitate cooking by open fire in the center of the circle. The fire was ablaze and gently burning to make coals for tonight's meal. All was at peace and harmony. A look of permanency permeated the area. Who would think that trouble could visit this land so soon in the future? Evidently, no one, as the mood that evening was one of relief and gaiety with some levity thrown in for good measure. Peaceful sleep came easily.

CHAPTER SIXTEEN

The next morning everyone found a type of excitement to see the planet's sunrise over what was thought to be the east. Even the usual sleepy heads were up and ata-em at the breakfast meal. Evie and Gloria were preparing it. There was bacon that had been irradiated a year ago. It tasted as though it were smoked only yesterday. Eggs fresh from the penned chickens they had ferried on board. They were now comfortably in a special pen for the animals. The pens were designed and constructed largely by Gloria, with Whisper helping.

The two married ladies, Gloria and Evie, made fresh coffee and topped off the meal with piles of pancakes made in an old ancient iron skillet. It was a treat after so many meals prepared in microwave ovens. The crew gave the two chefs a round of robust applause in appreciation. Then the explorers talked about plans of exploration and adventure, subject of course with the Captain's approval.

"This area is ideal for a camp, but how about something of a more permanent nature?" Rod Wheeler was one to get to a place more fitting for exploration of the archeological nature. He continued with only amenity in his voice. "Up a major river or on the side of a mountain might be better suited for permanent habitation," exclaimed Rod. "I had hoped to find some proof of sentient life on this most suitable planet. But, it would most likely be in the interior instead of near this coastline." A few groans of dissent were heard by those settled in for the long haul.

Rusty rubbed his chin, ran his hand over his face, and gave his usual smirky smile as he formed a responsible answer for Rod.

"I think I can concur with you Rod, except that most great centers of civilizations on earth was established on the coasts Here we landed in a different place than I first thought would present the best of all conditions for colonizing as well as a place that could be desirable for any past civilizations. My plans included a few days of rest and acclimation and then afterwards to return to the ship for a closer look at other landmasses. I know we all wanted to land promptly which we did. In addition, our landing direction was altered slightly because of the ship's computer's baffling numbers. Now, we can be more selective and be careful to locate a place that would facilitate most all of our needs. I think a two-day rest, would benefit all of us. Just relax for the two days after which we will load up and diligently explore the planet for the ideal location for exploration and colonization." Rusty finished by leaning back in his chair and indicating to Joel to continue with any other areas of concern. Every one was content with the program set forth by their leaders and eased into a more affable atmosphere.

The weather was very cooperative. Sunny skies with warm southerly; breezes were the order of the day. The animals also enjoyed the out of doors with crowing, scratching, strutting, by the chickens, rabbits and pigs. Two small goats ate every thing in sight. The men made up a game of basketball using a barrel hoop for the basket. The person on board the space freighter was Sparks. He was constantly searching with sensors for any possible sentient radio traffic as well as scanning the heavens for any moving life forms in space ships, such as Comet Chasers.

The two days of rest and relaxation passed very quickly. Jogging, game playing and just hanging was the order of the two days. At end of that time, the entire kit and caboodle was packed up and stowed aboard the freighter for further exploration. All were eager to leave because the weather was changing by a northerly blast of cooler air. It was surmised that at this location, wintry dying blasts were showing up. Only Pep was hesitant to leave since he had not sniffed out every nook and cranny in the region.

When all was on board including Pep, the big freighter lifted off the surface and cruised above the clouds at sub light speed to travel around the unusual equator. The southern hemisphere was much warmer because of the sun's position in the sky. Once in the air, all of the crew was straining to see an appropriate landing site. The geography was fascinating.

Eryka cried out that she saw movement and verified it by using infrared elecnoculars. Eryka Walther had spied movement of a warm body in a copse on the side of a hill miles ahead of the spacecraft. Eryka gave a running report as she kept her eye on the warm object.

"It appears to be an upright body moving much like a humanoid, on two feet," said Eryka. "Maybe we will find our cousins here, after all."

"Finally, extra terrestrial life," exclaimed Dr. Wheeler. "Where exactly is it? Can we land there?"

Rusty was also excited as the craft slowed down and began to hover over the suspected area.

Eryka continued with her report. The image was no longer in her view, but she was certain of the location.

"I think I lost the image over at that area of big trees. A little more to the port side and closer to the river where the image disappeared."

Rusty eased the big ship down to a clearing that was larger than several football fields. All eyes were fastened to the place where Eryka had seen her infrared image. Rusty gave every one warning about possible animals of unknown temperament just as they were cautiously disembarking.

Joel and a few of the men started to run with weapons on stun, towards the copse where the image was last seen. On entering the sheltered tree area, they found no person or animal. Rod was examining the ground for any sign that could help in their investigation. Joel was also on his knees, looking for anything that was out of order or any disturbed material. All of the members came up empty. Joel had even looked up into the trees for any life form that would inhabit the big tree's canopy. The search crew gathered and returned to the ship in a dispirited mood.

Rexanne was in a very blue mood, heard talking to no one in particular.

"I can't believe we were that close to a living being here. Maybe we should have searched longer. I have so wanted to be one of the first to make contact with any sentient species to examine and to try to communicate with."

Joel was quick to reply, "maybe next time, Doc. We will want to find a definite permanent camp and get well organized to make searches and do explorations. I am certain that our captain will appoint you as one of the leaders on future searches."

Returning to the big ship, they were met by questioning crewmembers concerning any luck on finding what Eryka has spotted earlier. After several minutes of comparing notes, Captain Bolt requested all crewmembers to reenter the freighter. Rusty had found what appeared to be a perfect site close by. He exclaimed the spot was close to a large body of water as well as a large river flowing into it. The place appeared on the geoscope to be fairly level with a few small hills behind the area. High ground was always a first choice of explorers for visibility and possible defense location.

When the ship finally landed at the appointed spot, the crew exited the freighter and began to select sights for various explorations. The animal pens were positioned close but not too close to the center of the selected areas by Gloria and Whisper. Sparks Walther set up a small work area where he could be close to the ship with electrical and sensor equipment. Rexanne had erected a tent that would serve as a first aid station with only a few essentials, leaving the more complicated medical apparatus and supplies on board. Rod had removed all stops in assembling his gear in a prefab hut that would serve as his base of operations. He was sure that he could find a place to explore with his trowels, shovels, picks and screens.

Eryka had brought sensitive equipment to monitor the atmosphere, pressure and temperature, wind, relative humidity and other kit to bring weather reports to the assemblage. Midge and Dirk were working in tandem setting a workstation that would serve both of their callings. Midge, with all of her special paraphernalia and Dirk with chemicals and bottles, flasks, and testubes made quite a show of teamwork and a visual orchestration of talents. Rusty and Joel had set up a command center on the fringe of the giant horseshoe shaped settlement. All was erected as before but with a lot less excitable enthusiasm.

Tables and chairs were set about as the final shelter was placed on the habitat's horseshoe-like configuration that also contained the mess. A kitchen for all seasons and palates. Naturally, all available hands had a part in its construction as food was on their mind after a busy day.

The rest of the day was used making final touches on all the shelters, as they would be used for sleeping quarters. Each occupant was responsible for their own equipment and any security that would be needed in their individual abode.

The group gathered at the dining mess and enjoyed a full course victory dinner, prepared by Whisper, Evie, and Gloria. A meal screaming for blue ribbons. Served up not as a duty but as joyful ritual. The meal was simply marvelous, considering we are billions of light years at a distance from the food's origins. When the dinner had finished, Rusty rose to make an announcement.

"We have come a long way. A distance never dreamed of only a few decades ago, before MacPherson's Arch was discovered. We now have broken a lot of barriers but must take a very serious look at the future here. It would seem unlikely that we could ever return home with limited fuel and supplies. With that in mind we must determine what season we are in here. If we find it conducive to planting we must make preparations for planting and allow the animals to mingle and produce offspring, something Midge will give us a foretaste in the near future." The group all looked at the new mother to-be and gave smiles and accolades in good fellowship.

It got quiet as Sparks gave out a report that he had scanned and registered a craft coming towards their planet. "It would take the craft sighting six or seven days to reach this general area. It probably is a Comet Chaser."

That made all the group look for some seltzer tablets.

CHAPTER SEVENTEEN

Lambert Bright was having the time of his life. He was in charge, and the old counselor was still far behind. Lambert could only surmise since not a sign of the Comet Chaser One had been reported. All sensors gave no indication that Battle Winslet had been able to repair his ship and continue after Lambert and his crew.

Comet Chaser Two was not having any mechanical problems, as was Comet Chaser One. Lambert and Garner Trapp were each fastidious about checking and rechecking all systems on a continuous basis. Garner, the electronic wizard made scans day and night to try to find out if Battle Winslet were still on course and to determine if the freighter they were chasing was still in range. Garner had fleeting images of the freighter ahead of them and nothing of the Comet Chaser probably behind them.

Lambert had his hands full keeping the passengers mollified and busy doing all kinds of tasks, both essential and non essential. Idle hands are the devil's playground, thought Lambert as he had one or more members take an inventory of all the food stock. A very important task really. The older men had a difficult time taking orders from young Lambert, but his voice and demeanor was such that they obeyed readily. The ladies on board continued to rearrange everything in the living quarters, which they made into separate places from the original dormitory style. They were enjoying the tasks with feminine vigor. The whole process took about two months but when finished it was a wonder to behold. Lambert's quarters were separate but because he was single, the ladies had placed a multiplicity of extraneous items in his living space. All in all the entire galactic cruise had started as a peaceful and busy atmosphere to the surprise of most on board.

It was during the third month that Lambert and his first mate, Garner Trapp, had to negotiate a truce between two men of equal rank. Battle must have chosen them because they were special friends of his. They had no unique talents and were barely of an age to intelligently procreate once in the colony on the new planet. Their names were Riley Striker and Bristle Fume. They were once commanders in the Galactic Air Navy. Each tried to carry a pose of command, especially when Lambert (now the Captain) gave an order. Bert tried not to make it a command but the hesitancy of the two required an authoritative military edict. When Lambert showed the slightest partiality to one of them the other fussed and ranted to the Captain. When the Captain gave a task to one the other complained.

"Why can't I do that?"

"He gets all the good jobs"

"That' not my duty."

"I can do a better Job than he."

On and on it went until one twenty-four-hour period the two antagonistic men got into a knot of fisticuffs. When

Lambert was apprised of this event, he and Garner separated the two men. Lambert cautioned each participant that if this occurred again he would put one or both in the brig, a small and cramped place set aside for just such an incident. With much grumbling and murmuring the two lieutenants parted with a handshake, demanded by Lambert. (The two were no longer Commanders since discharged under clouds of suspicious behavior and leaving their military post.)

After this bit of excitement, the cruise went more smoothly. Garner was busy trying to determine if fine-tuning regulators and fusion injectors could purchase greater speed and distance. It also was in his thinking to move into the perfect edge of MacPherson's Arch to maximize the Comet Chaser's speed and distance. A feat that would require the most delicate of calculations and maneuvering.

Lambert felt that his new calculations should place them on the edge of the Great MacPherson's Arch to increase movement and distance. Bert and Garner pored over charts and posed suppositions until they were dog-tired. Each man had different views on accomplishing the maneuver. Finally, Lambert yielded and stated that Garner was the flight expert and they would try his plan first. If it didn't produce, the desired results in could be rectified in about a week's worth of maneuvering. A small price to pay for excellence and perfection. Finally, the two gave their approval to Garner's numbers and then punched them in a very special, required sequence. This was accomplished by both voice commands and verification responses. The pilot's bridge sounded like a cacophony of choruses while a few older Commanders were heard grumbling negatives between verses.

When all of the new calculations had been programmed into the craft's computer all that was left was for Garner to activate it. When he pushed in the proper button, nothing seemed to happen, immediately. However, the gauges and sensors that Garner had calibrated carefully several times, showed the changes were happening to the satisfaction of Lambert. Moving to the edge of MacPherson's Arch, eventually, caused all sensors to come back to life in proper settings. The grumbling background was less vocal but still could be felt. It would take many hours of constant evaluations to see whether the move had accomplished the sought after goal.

Comet Chaser Two, a rather new ship with some very sophisticated apparatus that required a closely maintained exact temperature through out the ship. This being a constant job for Bonnie Gale when not attended to her other duties. Bonnie, the wife of Victor with appropriate training in complicated refrigeration too. Therefore, the job was most suitable for her. She must test the tanks, pumps, seals, and coolant lines daily to keep the temperature stable. The engines were proving to be very delicate but efficient.

One twenty-four-hour period the temperature began to fluctuate causing an alarm to sound. Bonnie ran to the controls to compensate the changes happening. She was a very conscientious lady. When she got to the control area, she found Bristle Fume frantically trying to alter the coolant flow without any success. Bonnie Gale asked Bristle to vacate her chair so she could adjust the controls to steady the temperature. He was argumentative and unwilling to surrender the chair; therefore, she called for security. Garner came to her aid and ordered Bristle to get up and leave the area immediately or he would clap him in the brig. It was a tense moment, but finally the younger man obeyed the older man, grudgingly. Bonnie on regaining her rightful position managed to stabilize the coolant in a very short time. When his friend and copilot told Captain Lambert of this incident, he ordered Bristle to the brig. This order obviously was not to be carried out with any ease. It took two other crew members to usher Bristle to the Brig, along with his great protestations. Lambert gave him two days in the brig with bread and water. In addition, if he didn't quiet down, Lambert said he would make it a week.

"I'll have no discord on my ship and if it takes long tours in the brig I can oblige anyone who disturbs the peace on my ship."

After that event, the ship's members seemed to settle down and be more compliant than ever. Lambert may be young but he is fair and stern; was the consensus from the other crewmembers.

The entire crew gave Garner , numerous compliments after formulating his new calculations and maneuver that gave the ship a three percent advantage over their previous positioning. Captain Lambert told him that they would arrive at their planned destination several days earlier than originally planned.

With this change in speed and velocity, Lambert was more confident than ever. He thought his ship would encounter the errant freighter first, showing Battle Winslet that young Lambert was a confident and capable officer and would be a tremendous asset in the colonization process quickly coming to pass. Lambert, now called Bert by one and all, was the first to exclaimed that the outer reaches of MacPherson's Arch was in sensor scan which meant a landing in about seven days. The excitement was high and contagious. Many members were bragging about how much land they would appropriate. An event Bert was also looking forward to the new possibilities ahead.

CHAPTER 18

The planet was all the colonizers had hoped for. Clear running rivers with lush grassy hills. The breezes reminded every one of spring. The great sea was only a short distant down the hills and was of a salty nature. An ample tide and blue color. Sea creatures were caught, studied, and carefully eaten to the surprise and gratitude of everyone. The fish were very much like the kinds on earth with unusual colors and fins in greater abundance. They contained skeletons that resembled the earthly counterparts with one exception. The rib cage was one continuous bony mass, not individual ribs like on earth. Flying creatures which were called birds because that is what they resembled were seen quite often and of varying sizes.

The group had settled in very nicely with all of the different couples having snugs of their own. A security detail of three teams was chosen by lot to keep an eye on land, sea, and sky. This duty was a rotating responsibility. According to their most recent scans, they all knew that visitors of dubious natures would be arriving in a few days so all were in a state of readiness for that event. Comet Chaser and its company might present difficulties not anticipated.

The men were also making forays into the great wooded area seeking signs of humanoid presence. Each day the reports were the same. "No signs today."

'Nothing of any importance had been discovered except a few spurious broken twigs or disturbed brush. Maybe an animal of some kind.

When Sparks gave the alarm that one of the vessels they thought was pursuing them was getting to the place of coming out of hyperspace and speed, they knew there was no sense trying to hide. The vessel's infrared and Ray-Wave sensors would locate any warm-blooded beings on the surface, and consequently, they would land close by. The sensors gave Sparks an ionic signature of a Comet Chaser. A medium size spacecraft with limited offense armaments and accommodations. The vessel had cramped living quarters and amenities. The occupants will be testy and mean after so long a journey. The group of adventurers gathered with what little weapons they possessed out of sight. They decided to show the incoming pursuers they presented no real threat. The colonists assumed the landing to be near a clearing that was so close to their New Hope settlement. They all heard the loud POP of the craft's deceleration to sub light speed and stiffened their resolve. They would not be intimidated or chastised in any manner. Whisper had volunteered to be the spokesperson for the first contact. Waiting was the hard part as they strained their ears for any sign of the Comet Chaser, coming around the planet for a slower approach. After what seemed to be hours, the group began to formulate a plausible reason of not being discovered. The consensus formulated, that the craft had lost its ability to make perfect infrared and Ray-Wave reading scans. Consequently, they quit and landed somewhere else on the planet. This explanation, even if a supposition, was received with relief and ebullience.

One by one, the group moved back to their respective snugs and continued the work they set out to do. They cut great logs from the woods to make dwellings that are more permanent. It was hard work. The entire group spent hours reviewing books and videodiscs about the subject. The crew became very amicable helping each other as the occasion presented itself. In the evenings, certain couples volunteered to present skits or mini plays for the enjoyment of all. Sometimes it was a comical production, and sometimes it was a musical. Four of the men soon had developed a very accomplished barbershop quartet. Eryka Walther was joyfully in her element.

The days passed pleasant enough, but the group kept wondering about the other spacecraft and where did it land. Could it have crashed? If that was the case, Rusty and Joel decided to conduct a meticulous but protracted search, and rescue by taking the freighter up for a look-see even with limited sub-light fuel. Of course, the entire group wanted to go along, leaving their settlement without any security. The group had formulated a democratic government that voted on all complicated or divisive actions. Rusty still led, but the vote was often used. This time the vote was that all would go, since no sign of incursion or offensive forces had been detected since coming to this place. Only Rusty wanted to leave someone behind for security. Rod Wheeler volunteered and would stay behind to allay the fears of the Captain. Pep was to also stay behind with Whisper's permission. After the vote, the group entered the freighter taking with them some bare necessities to help in any unusual discovery. Looking back at the nearly deserted little settlement they all left with a feeling of disquiet in their hearts. Few thought of unwanted guests. Home was now on the surface. The couples made themselves comfortable in their old quarters as they waited for Rusty to lift off the surface and begin the search patterns so assiduously taught at the Space Academy. All noses were pressed against port holes visibly scanning every nook and cranny on the surface that would come into view. Sparks was flipping dials and calibrating sensors and scanners to a fine-tuning edge. Rod had waved goodbye, as Rexanne had second thoughts about leaving her husband behind.

The scenery was more breath taking than other trips around the bulbous planet. Great canyons and rivers were in abundance. The Northern Hemisphere was more akin to the topography of North America and presented many livable areas for pleasant habitation. When Rusty took the freighter down under the bulbous equator, it was another story. There, the terrain was rough with mountains volcanoes , deserts, and vegetation of enormous size and thickness. The area had dozens of volcanoes, some active, and some in latent stages. The southern hemisphere exhibited a yellow brown haze from all the thermal activity. This was noted by sensors to have a mild toxic effect for humans. The area was much warmer in relation to the Northern Hemisphere. At the pole, the cap was covered with ice but also a few inactive volcanoes. With all of this information recorded in the ships computers, Rusty pulled the ship back up in the Northern Hemisphere and its more agreeable climate and terrain.

Eryka was almost beside herself with her climate recording sensors and computers. The pretty lady with the symmetrical face and soft eyes was using as much of her knowledge and equipment as the limited time would allow. Her dark hair would occasionally fall about her face but with quick movements, she put the offending wayward hair behind her ears.

"I have so many measurements to put in my report that will give us all an advantage in the climate department. I think spring is coming to our place."

Eryka spoke with no one in particular but all listened as though spoken to directly. Speaking to Rusty, she confirmed his suspicions.

"The southern hemisphere was going into winter and the northern was beginning spring and summer. The southern had many wild fluctuations of temperature and atmospheric composition. The Northern Hemisphere was more conducive to temperate climates and the southern had erratic swings of temperature and moisture content. Selecting the northern part of the planet is more conducive to our way of life with all the usual advantages of a mid planet temperate zone. This certainly a Cinderella planet even if the Southern hemisphere would present multiple problems if colonized."

Rusty agreed with her and her readings. He brought the freighter into a great arch that would take them back to the more temperate zone. Not finding the Comet Chaser was a mild set back, but Rusty was not deterred. Passing over the bulbous equator the infrared sensors registered a group of warm-blooded objects far below. Rusty took the spacecraft into a height of twenty Km where their presence would not be noticed. Hovering in space the crew managed all of the sensors and scans on the terrain far below.

"The objects below give a signature of humanoid forms," said Joel with excitement hidden in his voice. He was adjusting all of the scans for a close up of the captured images.

Just then, Sparks gave out a shout of discovery. "I have found a Comet Chaser on land just to the right of the humanoids. Maybe a few Km away. My electroscope has the ship and its passengers still inside with some confusion as though they landed only a short time ago. Their scan might have interpreted the humanoids as our little group supposed earlier and they landed close by to effect some sort of discipline or chastisement on us."

Rusty put the ship on autopilot as he examined all of the recordings and gave critical scrutiny to each one.

"You're right Sparks. The Comet Chaser crew has not disembarked yet for some unknown reason. I don't think the Chaser is damaged or disabled in any fashion. Joel, how low can we go down before the Chaser would spot us?"

"Boss, since we are directly over them it would be unlikely they would scan straight up and detect us. I think we could drop to about ten Km and be safe from detection." Joel bit his lip as the weight of command momentarily fell on his shoulders.

Gloria was chomping at the bit to land and discover the identities of the humanoids. Evie and Midge also had an over powerful urge to get down and begin studies and revelations of something so unique in their lives it was hard to sit still.

All of the on board crew pondered. Why did the Comet Chaser choose the equator to land at? Was it Chaser One or Two?

Rusty dropped the space ship down to 10 Km and settled into a hover over the Comet Chaser. When the sensors were engaged, Joel could not locate the humanoid images that had been on his screen just moments before. Sparks at his console also reported that no humanoid images were received, in fact nothing important was detected when the sensor's images came back, except the apparently confused crew of the Comet Chaser. Sparks had been keeping an eye on the Chaser for any suspicious movement. Only a positive report of life on board the craft. No orderly movement outside the vessel. The consensus of the Hope Merchant was to descend and examine the Chaser for any damage and to try to find the cause of its strange situation. Some of Rusty's crew volunteered to find any clues to the whereabouts of the detected humanoid apparition. Rusty decided to take the freighter down for a closer inspection of several unusual anomalies.

CHAPTER NINETEEN

Bert Bright was not a stranger to complications. He had led several very difficult missions before this long journey. It must have been one of the reasons Battle Winslet had chosen him to pilot the Comet Chaser II. He also had been intricately involved in several firefights on earth as his baptism as an officer and a gentleman.

Lambert or Bert as his friends called him was raised on a farm in the middle country of North America, in the region that was once the United States. His education was dispensed from a public school but with very high standards. Bert's parents were included in the lower classes, and it seemed as though their son would also be destined to that same strata unless by some good fortune he could climb into the higher classes by education, personality, and determination. The population of earth had migrated to be made up of two great classes. The low class and the high class. Middle class had just evaporated over the centuries, as one world government became the norm. Bert was one of the lucky ones, with high grades and an effervescent personality he was able to move up the ranks and joined the privileged.

He brought with him his humble beginnings and exercised passion and justice when necessary or required. His education was wide and varied to include many disciplines that would be needed in the life of a space officer. Bert had no time for relationships of the kind most young men sought. Few girls or dates were included in his activities. His main endeavor as a young man had been to better himself by education and an association with people of an ilk like his own, or higher. This had worked for him very well up to this point of his life.

The members in his Comet Chaser had endured a very tiring and difficult year in space. The artificial gravity was very poor on a Comet Chaser. The library and recreation area were meager at best so that the group mostly played cards and other games. This didn't sit well with players of average skills. Other events requiring space became annoying as one would bump into or require another's space, which created only nasty remarks and provoked angry relationships. All of the ship's amenities were at the saturation point. With only two sleep pods for stasis, the crew had scant opportunity for sleep privileges to wile away many of the tedious days. They all yearned for home and comforts left behind on a dying earth. Shades of the Hebrews leaving Egypt.

Only Garner Trapp stood by Bert's side when things got arduous. The two men now faced a group of unhappy, disgruntled, miserable people. The disagreement began to accelerate when Bristle Fume measured the living quarters. He had found that some of the cabins were slightly larger than others. This gave him ammunition to report to his cohort Riley Striker about this disparity of accommodations. Slowly the discontent spread like hot butter on toast until most of the members were measuring their own cabins for any slight disparity that might be present.

"The smaller cabins are for us less important persons," stated Bristle with a smirk and poison in its content to anyone that would listen, especially Bert. "People are upset about being assigned smaller cabins and want to be reassigned." Discontent oozing from the man with only guile in his heart. "You can't put me in the brig for commenting about our cramped quarters. It is my right." Bristle's utterances were cast with a snarl on his face and his soul.

Bert took it all in stride and only mentioned he was the captain on this ship and could take what ever measures were required for a safe and orderly journey. In addition, where would the reassignments go? All cabins are occupied. This quieted the disgruntled man for a while but Bert was aware that the man was trying to ferment trouble, so Bristle could take over and command the expedition without the classic mutinous scene.

Looking at Bert with a childlike utterance, "your cabin is bigger than mine, just because you are piloting this ship. How about giving me your cabin for the balance of the journey? Moreover, you have no companion to take up needed space leaving you an exorbitant amount of room I could use. These cramped quarters I'm in are making me slightly irritable."

Bert was certain that Bristle was more than slightly irritable but was not going to let him or his sidekick, Riley Striker, upset the entire group for one minute. His plan was to keep the cantankerous ex-commanders busy so they would be out of the way.

"Tell you what, Bristle, if you and Riley would measure all the cabins down to the last centimeter and record your findings after signing the report for future official examination, I might reconsider the cabins assignments to your advantage. You must get each cabin's occupants willingness to give you a signed release to enter the cabins for size determination."

The two troublemakers left with a gleeful smile on their faces. Bert hoped the entire process would take a long time. The only other solution was to put both miscreants in sleep stasis at the same time. The measuring process should be strung out on the basis that the two would sign the report and expect it to be seen by higher up officials, if not now, someday. Close to the targeted planet gave Bert a sigh of relief.

Bert tried to inform the others that much of the journey was completed and they could be planning on their arrival and subsequent occupation of new lands. This bit of encouragement had its effect so that Garner and Bert could get back to the delicate operation of a Comet Chaser in deep space.

"How much longer will we be on MacPherson's Arch," asked Garner? Bert was quick to reply.

"My estimation is in about a month at the least. My calculations give us only a flexible few hours of miscalculation so I thought you, and I need to go over all of the figures one more time while we can. It also appears that our Battle Winslet is not in scanner range, or he has returned to earth. This gives us pause to rethink any kind of confrontation we might have with the freighter Hope Merchant's crew and officers."

Garner was surprised to hear his friend talk about confrontation when he knew Bert to be an individual of moderation and embraced the confines of reason. He wanted to ask more questions about this but knew they had much work to accomplish before their arrival at the Hope Merchant's planet. Garner's only clue was that the Counselor had a daughter, Whisper by name, that was a stow-away on the freighter and that the Counselor was very disturbed about it. The Counselor's last transmission indicated that we were to apprehend the girl and try to keep her until Battle arrived. Garner knew Rusty Bolt by reputation and was certain that a confrontation with him was not in our best interest.

The next few weeks were filled with an array of emotions and minor conflicts as Bert and Garner laboriously piloted the ship to near perfection. Bristle and his friend Riley had measured almost all of the cabins to the last centimeter without any clear cuts report they were willing to sign. This exercise had fulfilled Bert's desire to occupy the malcontents until the planet was in range. It was take them to a near touch down that overshadowed any discontent of the part of the two complainers. The little ship was finally filled with excitement and relief as the expected POP of coming out of hyperspace and speed, resulting in coming off MacPherson's Arch. Seeing first hand, the new planet that Hope Merchant and Rusty Bolt found was dramatic.

Bert gave the countdown to exit the Arch's hyperspace and to begin to revolve around the planet at sub light speed. The countdown went smoothly, and the POP gave everyone the thrill they had anticipated. The ions, molecules, and energy of their bodies and surroundings came at the same time, as star lines disappeared. The planet was now in view from a great distance. All the viewers gave out sighs of relief and joy. Bert made the necessary passes and tried to locate the missing freighter.

When their scanners spotted life forms in a group, it was assumed that was the missing crew. The spacecraft eased down about a mile away from the humanoid infrared images. When they finally settled on the ground, the people of Chaser Two went berserk trying to exit the ship without any preliminary precautions and operations. Bert made them all wait with the help of a blaster threat. It was a blessing, the habitat was agreeable to human requirements, noticed Bert on the scans and gauges.

Bert and Garner had to stun some of the passengers to restore calm. When calm was restored, Bert returned to his console for further sensor testing and concluded that the images were not the freighters crew but a new humanoid species. This revelation was kept to only Bert and Garner, as the others were too excited to be told about any unexpected development. When all had been returned to some semblance of order Bert wanted to tell all of the members one more time what he expected them to do. Advances and explorations were to be made slowly and with deliberate purpose. Order was very important, as was documentation of everything new or puzzling. They all had to be fitted with special suits in case the environment was not completely favorable. A Galactic Exploration and Search cautionary requirement. Many of his group had not prepared with their suits and air masks. A fight broke out between those that had prepared and those that had been in such a hurry that they did not suit up. The unprepared, led by Bristle and Riley, were in such a frenzy to be first out that Bert and Garner had some of the more prepared to confine these two miscreants to the small brig under great and vitriolic protests.

All of this confusion and unacceptable behavior cost the group much time. When all were in readiness, Bert disclosed that all the images captured earlier had vanished from the ship's sensors.

"I don't know for certain what this new development means, but I must caution each and everyone not to venture far from the ship and be prepared for any offensive contingency. This planet is full of unknowns so be very careful in what you touch, see, or hear. The intercom in your helmet is to be used sparingly and quietly so others can also report and understand the communications as they find something to report. I want all to wait outside by the exit until everyone has assembled."

The entire process of fights, suiting up and exiting took over an hour but finally completed at sunset. A sunset of rare beauty with golds, pinks, and purples fused with yellows and stabbing whites with an azure background so vivid that it assaulted the eyes and brain.

CHAPTER TWENTY

The big freighter kept its place in the stratosphere and continued to monitor the events far below. When it was apparent, the Hope Merchant could detect nothing further of importance at this height, Rusty eased the freighter down to a position between the Chaser and the first sighting of humanoids. This was far away so that they were not easily seen. This took all the piloting skills that Rusty could muster. The clearing was about the same size as the freighter, allowing Rusty with close sensor readings to land away from any exiting of crew from the Comet Chaser. In sensor range but not visible. The big ship settled down without a bump or a bang to the credit of Rusty Bolt and Joel Kerr.

"Gently as a Baby placed in his crib, uttered Joel.

The first order of business was to continue to scan both the Chaser and the copse where the humanoid images had been recorded. This was the job and joy of Sparks who was in his glory as the electrical wizard. The sensor array's had to oscillate to keep both targets in a registering position.

When nothing of any movement was observed, concerning the humanoids, Sparks gave the go ahead to the other crew members to exit with care.

"Everything looks good for us to exit," said Sparks with the voice of confidence mastered over years of experience. Rusty and Joel led the little expedition out into the heavy vegetation towards the Comet Chaser. Sparks and Rexanne stayed behind to guard the ship. Whisper was in the lead with Pep pulling her forward on his leash. Slow down Whisper," advised Rusty. "We are in very strange conditions and surrounded by unknown terrain."

"I just want to see if the Comet Chaser is the one my family might be in. I want to be the first to greet the people my father chose to make this historic flight. They will be less angry with me than you, Captain."

Whisper and Pep moved through the trees and bushes with apparent ease. Pep making constant sniffing observations just a few feet in front of his mistress.

Rusty remembered that Whisper had told him about getting her dog, earlier in the flight. When Whisper was just a teenager, she longed for a friend or confidant. Her parents were opposed to an animal of any kind so Whisper was in a constant melancholy over this dilemma. A friend suggested she try prayer. It was an old form of petitioning but not one that was forgotten. Whisper would have to petition God for this dog-getting favor and respond by being a person practicing righteousness. It was a difficult procedure, as her family like many others in the space service didn't go to church or believe in a God of omnipotent powers. Many nights by her bedside on her knees, Whisper began to develop a relationship with this divine personage, until finally she was as sure of His existence as she was of her own. With this blossoming relationship growing, it became very apparent to Whisper that her asking privileges were dependent on her obedience to things in a book, long unread in her house. When she had graduated from school, her grandmother gave her this book called the Bible. It was placed on a lower shelf in the library so as not to embarrass the up and coming Battle Winslet. Whisper ultimately had read this book through and bent her will towards its teachings and commandments. It was this preparation and practice that Whisper confessed, led her to have her Pep. When talking to her father about her desire to have a dog one night, he jokingly said if a puppy dog came out of the sky, he would permit Whisper to keep it. Soon after Battle's partial softening, Whisper had responded to a fire siren close-by and went to see the fire. Whisper settled under a low hanging roof of the building close to the fire. Not too close to the flames. She was privy to all of the fire fighting by the attending firemen. Unknown to her, the mother dog had given birth to puppies weeks earlier in the house on fire. When the fireman noticed the dog and pups, he got all of them, but one, out of harms way via a roof opening. The last puppy was saved by the fireman when the blaze had almost made it impossible to reach the puppies, but he did. In his hurry and frustration to save the pups, he cast the little dog up on the adjacent building's low roof. About this time, Battle Winslet was coming home and seeing his daughter standing back and watching the proceedings, he joined her by the protected low roofed building.

"Well daughter what can you tell me about this fire?"

Whisper raised her arms to point to the now distant flames and explained what she had seen so far. At that very instant the last saved puppy fell off the roof and into Whisper's waiting arms. Her father just looked with stunned amazement as Whisper pulled the little black, fury puppy into her arms and shouted. "Thank you Lord for this is my puppy and my answer to prayer."

Battle was speechless for he remembered his causal utterance in the past to the young girl. It was a statement that he thought impossible and could not happen. Whisper had seen the impossible in her spirit and now held the improbable in her arms. Her Father in heaven had answered her prayer.

Later, Whisper asked the people whose house had been on fire if she could keep the pup, and of course, the answer was "yes." In fact, they told her she was an answer to prayer because they no longer could keep all the pups because of the fire. It was a story that happened to a teenage girl long ago and some of it was sometimes forgotten but not the important part Whisper admitted to Rusty.

"But it really happened. Miracles still happen," were her concluding words.

Looking at the girl now was a pleasant sight thought Rusty. Her confidence and love for that dog was very touching and moving.

The forward group was gaining ground at a rapid pace with Pep and Whisper pulling through the trees and luxurious vegetation. They would soon be out of the woods and be exposed to the Comet Chaser's crew.

Rusty used his infrared elecnoculars. He suddenly raised his hand for the group to halt for he'd registered human images just ahead. Everyone halted but Whisper who unknowingly swept ahead with only Pep for company. Rusty opted to not call out and betray their position. He motioned for the others in his group to lay low and by gestures signaled he was going ahead by himself.

All of Rusty's senses were at his highest discerning levels, moving forward as silently as a soft breeze. He could see Whisper now about twenty meters ahead. She had her head down and was squatting down with Pep by her side. She had spotted the group ahead of her. Humans no doubt in full space gear. They were having a difficult time of it. Walking slowly with heads in a down position not observing too much in the way of what lay ahead. Whisper stayed in a crouched position until the head person was almost upon her, Giving Pep the opportunity to emit a low and deep growl of menacing proportions. The lead person spotted the dog first and began to raise his weapon for a stun shot. Whisper was up and out like a shot, throwing her full weight on the offending shooter. The rest of the advancing group all retreated a few paces. At this point, the lead person tore off his helmet and gazed in to the eyes of the most determined and lovely orbs he had ever seen. His words came out strong and clear.

"Don't shoot anybody. She is a friend and not a foe as you can well see. I think I was floored by an angel." Bert was smitten like a lightening bolt.

Whisper came up and held Pep on a tight lease, as he wanted to finish his security job. The other Chaser members were taking off their helmets as they could see and now believe the atmosphere was acceptable for human adaptability.

Rusty was watching all of these proceedings from a vantage point not too distance from their origins. Very slightly, he could feel the others in his group moving forward after he had signaled them to advance, unobserved. His plan was to wait and see what Whisper and Pep did before reveling themselves. He held his breathe as well his stun gun as he watched the Chaser group go through their discussions and salutations to Whisper Winslet. No Battle Winslet was going to be a big plus thought Rusty. The young lady had them in the palm of her hand with greetings and with profuse confirmations of their safety concerning the crew of the Hope Merchant. At this point, she disclosed that her group was close by and got permission from Bert to wave them in. Whisper held up her arm and waved her friends into the mostly friendly circle of humans.

Rusty advanced cautiously with stun gun at the ready by his side. When in the circle he introduced himself and the group that had accompanied him to this location. When all signs of possible hostilities had evaporated the group entered into lively discussions of old times and places. It was amazing to find that two groups had much in common. Friends of friends as well as places that many had been to in times gone by.

All of this camaraderie was without any talk of possible humanoids in the area. Rusty's crew was describing about places visited on the planet, thus far. Plans for the future was also on the agenda. Food supplies were very much in the conversation. After several hours of this kind of fellowship, the two leaders eased away from the gathering to discuss more plans that are serious.

Bert and Rusty hit it off immediately. Bert related about of his two troublemakers in his brig. Rusty said, "We have spotted some images of humanoids in this area, so be very careful. We want to find a final place for colonization away from any possible inhabitants."

"I am not sure if Battle is still coming, but in any case be on the lookout for him. I know he had trouble with his Chaser and might have gone back to earth or will still come on to try in Comet Chaser One. The talk went on for a lengthy period. The two leaders compared notes and separated to lead each group in a manner that best suited their respective members.

"Is the Counselor's daughter to stay with you or am I required to assume responsibility for her?" Bert spoke with mixed emotions in his voice. A man that had been stunned by her beauty and bearing. His heart beat hard, and his mouth became dry as he waited for Rusty's answer.

CHAPTER TWENTY-ONE

It was very difficult to give Bert an answer. Rusty knew Bert must be under some command or request to retrieve the daughter of Battle Winslet. "Whisper has become such an integral part of my group," said Rusty with some reluctance so as not to benefit his chance of Bert lessening his request for Whisper to join his group. Rusty and Bert agreed to ask Whisper with which group she would want to stay.

Bert thought about having to face Battle Winslet sometime in the future if the young woman chose to stay with a group that had displeased the Counselor. Rusty's mission had taken Battle by surprise. Battle wanted to lead this mission and be the first to discover a new world and other possible unique disclosures. Counselor Winslet also had visions of grandeur, wanting to set up a kingdom style government with Battle as King or magnate. Lambert Bright did not embrace his vision, but he would follow orders if they did not cross a moral line. 'Battle may never reach this planet thought,' young Lambert Bright.

The two men approached Whisper, who was having a lively discussion with Garner Trapp and friend. It was difficult to interrupt Whisper when she was in high gear but Bert managed a stifled cough, a clearing of the throat.

"May we speak to you in private, Miss Winslet?"

She smiled at Bert and targeted him with her piercing blue eyes.

"Certainly. If you will excuse me Garner and Fairly Trapp."

Fairly was the kind of woman that one thought would be the wife of a space plot. Tall and willowy as her husband, Garner. She was well versed in all subjects that one could bring before her. A woman that was gregarious and intelligent. She and Garner moved away in a subtle manner not belying that the group they had just left were in a confidential mode.

Rusty, her present benefactor and captain, put the question at hand candidly before her. "Which group would you like to stay with during the colonizing of this planet? Your father commissioned the Comet Chaser Two and Captain Bright as a vessel of possibilities and leader for this mission. Captain Bright has suggested he could include you in the roster of the Chaser Two if you so desired. The Hope Merchant's crew has grown close to you and Pep, having enjoyed a year of your presence. We would continue to give you and pep all the latitude that would be needed for a pleasant establishment of your home."

Bert made his plea in a stiff and official way the gave Whisper the complete freedom to made her choice without rancor or future retribution.

Whisper was no fool. She knew that this decision would affect her entire life. She had understood in all the conversations that the two groups might split up and settle in different parts of the planet. Only coming together on special occasions or emergencies. She had become acutely aware that no unmarried men were on the Hope Merchant. The Comet Chaser had a few unmarried men. One was of course, Lambert Bright. A good catch by any standard. On the other hand, she was very comfortable with the crew of Hope Merchant and a life of unwed existence might not be too bad. Her crewmates all got along with each other and her and Pep. She had heard rumors of two unsavory characters that Bert had to deal with some severity. She wouldn't want them in her backyard.

"Captain Bolt, would this decision be binding and inflexible. Could I for some reason choose another group at a later date?"

"Your decision is for convenience now, but later you could transfer into another group or go somewhere and live by yourself, if you chose. We need only an answer now so we can separate into the two groups and begin the process of colonizing this new planet."

Bert was holding his breath all during this dialogue to the extent that Rusty wondered if Bert was sick. Bert had deep feelings for the young lady and was wishing she would choose his company and ship. He remembered her when on earth, even though they were distant and or platonic observations. He was also aware he had no wife to make the colonizing process more appealing. He also knew that a single girl in the midst of many men could also be the focal point of trouble. Fallacious rumors and innuendoes could tear a mission apart with the rapidity of falling lightening. Bert had had a few girlfriends as a student but nothing serious. At the Academy, he had no time for dating as all of his energies and time went towards his academic career. Here and now, he would have a lot of time for spouse and family. With his hands in his pockets and the slow shifting of weight on his legs, Bert waited for an angel to make her decision.

"Captain, if you don't mind I would like to stay with you and Hope Merchant for the foreseeable future. At a later date, I might be persuaded to change my mind. I realize that being single may pose a problem with one group or the other, but the crew of the Hope Merchant has given me and my dog Pep every courtesy and consideration without complications. If my father eventually comes, he may have some eligible bachelors that would alleviate any pressures I see for the present. I know this may sound callous, but the truth being so much better than formal or punctilious thinking."

Bert took this statement as though a great weight had been placed inside his heart making it near the bursting point. He had not known which way she would want to go, but at the mention of eligible bachelors, his inner world began to crash. Bert hung onto the former words of Whisper.

"I might be persuaded to change my mind."

With this near dilemma, out of the way the two leaders had to make more decisions. Rusty and Bert had discussed about all of the difficulties facing this group of colonizers. One problem was Chaser Two's diminishing fuel supply. Rusty faced a similar situation. They would make exploring forays later and preferable together as long as fuel lasted. Rusty and Bert had discussed about all of the other difficulties facing this group of colonizers. It was decided that Bert and his group should find a place suitable for habitation and set up camp as soon as possible. They would make exploring forays later and preferable together if possible.

The two groups tested their respective communications com-link radios and set position points to coincide with agreed upon directions and compass points. The planet had a similar magnetic reference points that indicated a perfect north. When all of these preparations had been completed, the two groups gave a strained farewell. With arms waving and then a final dip by Bert's Comet Chaser the groups were again separated by a stillness no one had expected. Rusty gatherer his crew around him for a meeting of the minds.

"We know we saw very definite signs of warm blooded humanoids in this area, and it would be to our advantage to search for any signs to corroborate our findings. We will keep in one group for security and make ever-increasing circles beginning here on the fringe of the suspected zone; ending at the last place, we sighted the images. All weapons on stun only and be very slow in make any offensive gestures."

With these instructions, the group moved in every increasing circle, examining the ground or flora for any signs of habitation. Rusty and Joel led the expedition with Midge and Dirk close on their heels and Eryka on the outside. Evie and Gloria made up the rear. Whisper and Pep had returned to the freighter reuniting with Rod and Rexanne. After several hours, the searching group began to loose interest in the task.

Midge was picking up rock samples and had her nose to the ground. Midge loved her profession of being a geologist. She began in humble beginnings as had her husband Dirk. The pair was a study in opposites. She was short and plump with dark hair and heavy eyebrows but very gregarious. Midge met Dirk at school and began a courtship that defied description. Dirk was tall and thin with a long nose and large owl-like glasses. His studious demeanor was in conflict with Midge's devil may care persona. Midge was full of life going to parties and dances while Dirk hung back and watched or took notes on the activities. The pair was deeply in love as seen by much hand holding and speaking affable of the partner at all times. They also gave glances to one another that spoke of devotion and solidarity. Midge was the spokesperson for the couple as she was an extrovert. Dirk was not a sad sack by any means or an introvert of serious proportions. He could laugh and find humor in many instances so that no one could call him antisocial. Dirk had a deep almost ministerial voice that carried much authority; Midge had a high-pitched voice that still had the taint of childhood attached. These differences did not bother either party in their professional endeavors or in their marital cohesiveness. Her high-pitched voice rang out to unsettle tired eyes and poorly focused minds.

"I have found something!"

Midge had her head down close to the ground when she shouted. She was trying to lift a suspicious looking rock but could not budge it. Dirk was close at hand and was told by Midge that the rock was a bit of fakery. It appeared real to the untrained eye but Midge began to explain in detail her finding to Dirk. When Rusty and Joel arrived with most of the group, they inquired about this unusual find.

"Captain, this heavy rock is situated in the wrong place and has not the striations and content of a real rock of this region I have been studying."

"Midge what do you think the significance of this find is?"

Rusty was now kneeling on the ground with Joel, examining the rock with an acute assessment. Midge did not mince words as she spoke up with a certain degree of pride.

"I believe this is an entrance or trap door to an underground habitation."

CHAPTER TWENTY-TWO

This revelation was enough to pump adrenaline into every one in Rusty's group. Dirk was able to confirm his wife's find by moving the rock ever so slightly and seeing a dark space under the rock instead of dirt. The other giveaway was the absence of weeds around the rock's base. Dirk told Rusty the rock seemed to move on an axis or hinge. Rusty had everyone stand back from the object so that he and Joel could examine it more closely before trying to budge it. By now all tracks that might have been around the rock had been obliterated but Rusty still told Sparks and Evie to search the area farther out for any kind of tracks or impressions that would give them an idea of what lay below. Dirk was not to be denied as his wife's find was also his find in his mind. He wanted to be sure that the revelation was not tainted or compromised. Midge was right beside him and both of them were only an arms length away from the two leaders and their examination. Midge was giving an on going dialogue about the rock and its unusual construction. When everyone had examined the object Rusty and Joel with the help of Dirk, easily moved the rock in a levered fashion, exposing a hole and tunnel, complete with well worn rocks or steps. With stun guns at the ready and flashlights showing the way, the little group began the trip down into the opening. The stairs were wide and made of perfectly cut flagstone. The group bunched together and quietly listened for any sound that might give them a hint at what might exist below. To everyone's surprise the air was fresh and moving.

Joel had to say in Rusty's ear, "I hope we are not getting in over our heads," as the group moved down and under the surface. Rusty was only slightly amused. He continued down the stairs until they came to a level place with ornate walls. The corridor was wide but dark. There was a minute when all stopped to admire the decorated walls and try to decipher what they were seeing. The walls reminded Rusty of the passageways in the ancient tombs in far away Egypt. Signaling the group by hand signals, and flashlight waving the assemblage then moved forward into the bowels of this planet.

Rusty had reminded the group that if they met any unsuspecting humanoids they were to try to be as peaceful and compliant as vanilla custard. This could be accomplished, if no weapons were in sight or offensive movements by the residents were noticed, by raising their hands in the universal gesture of surrender. With this thought in the minds of the informed trespassers, it slightly impeded the alert forward progress. They were absorbed by the fascination of the beauty of the wall's scenes and caricatures. Because of this, progress was slow even though every ear was tuned to the front for any indication of life or movement.

Rusty felt he had spent his life preparing for this occasion. All of the years of training and studying were encapsulated in these moments. He had told Evie about his other exploits with a certain braggadocio quality that now might need some amendments. With Evie by his side, he was confident that what ever they found in this land under the surface, they together would survive and even overcome the obstructions and difficulties. His wife of only a bit over a year moved closer and closer as the moments dragged on, with Joel and Gloria close behind them.

Evie was absolutely certain she had made the right choice in accepting Rusty Bolt's bold marriage proposal over a year ago after only a brief courtship He was all she had every hoped for and more. A confident, caring man of varied abilities. A source for strength and wisdom and passion. She remembered as a child her dreams of a prince in shining armor coming for her and whisking her off to a fairyland. It was not quite that way, but in her mind, the entire dream had materialized and was coming true. A new land and life was before her to make and to mold in her own special way with the help and guidance of God. She could be nothing but happy and satisfied. What ever lay ahead was going to be to her and Rusty's benefit and joy. With those true and comforting thoughts, she came back to the passage and felt her husband's grip tighten.

"I think I hear something," whispered Rusty. Every one stopped and cocked their ears to the front of the passageway for a better opportunity to listen to a kind of murmur or undertone of strange voices. Looking ahead the group could see light and a large room with human-like figures walking about, keeping occupied in some manner or other. It was like an underground city with stalls, sheds, and hovels placed in a great circle.

Two occupants stood at the end of the tunnel as though they were guards. Since they were closest, Rusty noted in his mind their appearance. They were short and had hair in a stand up fashion. Mouths like ours he thought as one guard began to look and advance their way. They had flat foreheads, and large ears with noses built for smelling. Large round eyes, probably to accommodate this dark environment completed the facial appearance of these people. This combination gave the trespassers the comprehension that they were truly different and yet similar. The guards smelled them as they spied them in the dark passageway and gave out a warning shout of discovery. In a very short time, the passageway was swarming with the planet's inhabitants as the offending group raised their arms and hands in the universal sign of surrender. It was a chaotic few minutes as the intruders were met and bound by the residents. Many of which were quite affected by the appearance of the crew of Hope merchant. Some dropped what looked like spears and ran away; some just gaped in awe while some more bold in their actions and finally bound the explorers with root rope. Quite archaic but effective. Clubs and sharpened spears gave the Hope Merchant crew an idea of the minimal social progress of these persons.

When bound hand and foot the group was led hopping into the center of the underground village. There, the members of the village waited in dispassionate silence. After what seemed like an eternity of time, twelve of them came forward and stood before the little group of interlopers. These people reminded Rusty of tribal peoples of earth in centuries past. Intelligent but still in a state of unsettled purposes. They spoke with their mouths in a clicking, and guttural tone that was never heard on earth but rose and dipped with emotion and facial movements, leaving the prisoners in no doubt of the content. Unhappiness and anxiety moved across the villagers faces like a winter snowstorm, cold and sudden. Eventually, one person came forward, taller than the others; to be their spokesperson as Rusty was for the prisoners.

Rusty made every effort to placate his host with nothing but condescending gestures and language spoken softly. This kind of exchange went on for a long time, each trying hard to find out about the other without any immediate success. Rusty was sure that the inhabitants had seen them above ground and by gestures got the impression they knew of the space ships and Lambert Bright's group as well. When both representatives apparently ran out of steam, the prisoner's were led to a hovel that evidently was to be their prison while in this place. A hovel made of root material as was the body coverings of the underground people. It was like linen, made by scraping the roots to make a woody material that was spun and weaved into clothing.

Without the bindings being removed the group of eight were ushered in and gestured to sit down and wait. The guards left them and returned to the village center.

Evie and Gloria remarked how like a western scenario this situation reminded them of movies of long ago.

"It always turned out right in the end," stated Gloria that was her positive outlook on all things.

Of course, Evie had to agree as the others murmured only a faint assent.

CHAPTER TWENTY-THREE

The waiting, always the waiting to bear heavy on one's soul. Not knowing what was to happen next was a burden shared by many but only endured one at a time. The noises outside the hovel are what one would expect in a cheap novel. A commotion with ominous portends and creating visions of all kinds of distress. It appeared as though their captors were trying to decide method they would execute the prisoners.

Rusty was trying to extract some ideas from his group of trussed up crewmembers.

"I was thinking that the best way to communicate with these folks is through mathematics or even music," said Rusty as he tried to peer out the opening to see if any noticeable progress was being made by their captors "I expect they respect courage so keep your game faces strong and positive."

"It is very difficult to have a song in your heart when one is bound up like birthday present," responded the ever-humorous Joel.

The first thing that came into the head of Gloria was, "maybe I could sing a little ditty I learned at my mother's knee."

Joel responded to his wife's very astute suggestion. "You learned a good song at your mother's knee while I learned some unsavory traits at some other joint."

"This is a serious situation we are in," spoke Gloria with a softness reserved for her husband.

Midge just continued to cry softly as Evie was preparing to enter the conversation. "I think we must try to use diagrams in the dirt to explain what we are and what we intend to do or not do." A very wise comment by Evie as she strained against her bonds.

"These root binders don't help one to think very clearly. I think we must use all three kinds of communication to get through to these folks before we end up as the main attraction this day." Dirk was not inclined to frivolity but all could see his tense tether was forcing some levity from him. The man continued with a resignation in his voice. "I hope they loosen these ropes before they leave us to sleep or die."

Of course, the ladies all agreed with each other in principal as they asked Rusty to take a part in these concepts by getting the attention of one or another of the head men for a pow-wow and putting all of the voiced suggestions into play.

"The tall one in particular as he projected leadership," said Evie.

Evie and Gloria even volunteered to sing a duet to try to win over the hearts of their captors. After this was said and agreed upon, Rusty attempted to roll towards the door and began to shout for an audience of any important persons. It was met by some success as one small man with a root staff came to the door and whacked Rusty on the head. It was not a deadly blow but certainly a blow for quiet and understood immediately.

Several weary prisoners finally fell asleep in their cramped positions while others kept watch and attempted to wriggle free from the confining bonds. To little avail. These captors must have had some previous experience in holding captives. Some comfort was finally purchased by Rusty and Joel, but not for long.

Two larger men, broad shouldered and bigger than the other men came into the hovel and lifted Rusty and Joel to their feet and escorted them outside and into a circle of many indigenous beings. These people appeared by all standards very much like humans at home, that some called homely or craggy. Very sentient and with intelligence. Certainly not animal-like or unlearned.

Joel made the first attempt to sing a song. Surprisingly it was soft and sweet with words to match. All of the tribal band stopped their doings and looked at Joel with wondering expressions. From the hovel came a response by Gloria with sweet silky tones that made the captors look even more quizzical. At this point, a great debate took place among all of the tribal peoples, which eventually, ended by untying Joel and giving him nods of approval and continuation. Other root people entered the hovel and brought out one very surprised Gloria. She was also being unbound and to her credit, she continued to sing, responding to Joel's sonorous lyrics. It was a sight to behold. Men and women of another planet beginning to break into some sort of song and dance that was very pleasing and yet identifiable as story telling of long ago events.

One by one, the captives were brought out and unbound to enter the singing festivities. Rusty was busy at the dusty floor making signs and diagrams for the elders to examine with awe and some comprehension. The dusty revelations soon had some mathematics equations not recognizable by anyone except Rusty so he changed to simpler numbers. One plus two equals three. With this being recognized, it was assumed by all, that these two groups had similar understandings and all hostilities began to fade away.

Rusty indicated they would have to go up on the surface soon, but their hosts indicated they wanted to show off their underground habitat first. A few words were cast about and learned by each group in an attempt to better communicate.

The main host's name was something like click-up because he was taller than most of his contemporaries. Rusty gave them him a name of Leggs and the tribe he called Root People. They all seemed to like the sounds those words formed. With very much agreement, Leggs began to show off his underground paradise.

The reason they lived down here was because a band of sea people would come upon them regularly, take all their provisions, and sometimes even some of them as slaves. After many years of this kind of treatment. Legg's ancestors took a band people and went underground for protection. From this vantage point, they could go above ground when necessary but live underground with the roots. One great room Rusty and his crew were shown was the food room. Entering a small door with a thick root curtain covering, the Hosts ushered them into a mammoth room with a ceiling close to the surface. The room was arched with many timbers that supported the ceiling. A net made of loosely woven root material was below the arched timbers. Below was a pool of warm water that its vapors apparently lifted up towards the ceiling Growing on the ceiling was a fabulous variety of tubers. They pointed out what appeared to be potatoes, carrots, turnips, beets, and other harvestable foodstuffs for Legg's people. On secure days, the gardeners went on the surface and planted the tuber-like vegetables. Protein was gathered in the rivers, lakes, and forests when needed. The smoke from the living quarters was dissipated by a series of hollow timbers taking the smoke away from the main area and letting it exit under a near-by small water fall that make the smoke almost imperceptible. The complex was most intriguing and complete. The tour ended with handshakes and the exchanging of small gifts and pledges of blood and hugs. The entire time was about thirty-four hours and had exhausted everyone, but joyful emotions rose as another exit was shown the little group of former captives. They exited to the surface with a real expanded knowledge of these new world peoples.

CHAPTER TWENTY-FOUR

It was a very difficult job at best, for the two men on Comet Chaser One to fix and repair the fusion regulators and ionic plasma injectors. Walter was a wizard at these kinds of electrical and mechanical equipment. Carl was also a most experienced mechanic of space ship engines. The men repaired the engine and informed Battle Winslet that they could continue on their voyage on MacPherson's Arch.

The roster of Comet Chaser One was more to the liking of Battles' wife; Blenda. The crew was made up of younger people that were on Battles list of up and coming members of the Universal Galactic Flight Academy.

Blenda was trying to keep order among the ship's members by instituting games and even plays and mystery dinners. The accommodations were cramped, and the supplies very limited so that everyone had to get along to make the long journey tolerable. Rationing was never popular. Blenda became the center of all the social activities to the dismay of Battle. He was the kind that wanted his wife to only minister to his needs. This new situation caused Battle to become very gruff and short tempered.

Blenda didn't care and organized each person as a cast member of the Comet Chaser One thespians. Her plays were quite simple so that even Waver could participate. The best play was about a mystery of murder on the Orient Space Shuttle. A play Waver had suggested and Blenda spun it into a tale of inauspicious proportions. It was about a space shuttle that was taken over by an evil young man and his gang. Bart the evil young man had taken prisoner the daughter of the king of the orient, who was trying to get her back posthaste. The chase involved much dialog and theatrical flare. When the king caught the errant Bart, He found that someone had killed one of the king's guards, who had been hiding on board the shuttle. This guard was not able to keep the daughter safe for some medical reason of dubious import. Nevertheless, the guard had been murdered. Bart was brought up on murder charges and convicted to hang. On the appointed day of the execution, the daughter admitted the guard had tried to molest her and she foiled his attempts, and in the process, the man was killed in self-defense, thereby freeing Bart. Blenda interjected the last part to the consternation of Battle. This play kept the members interested in what they were about on this mission. Each presentation was mixed with some extemporaneous changes that dismayed Battle to no end because the alterations were against the King and for the errant Bart. (Maybe Waver?)

The weeks and months wore on in a never ending kind of hypnotic sea of sameness that began to get boring to more members that could be tolerated. Battle was always angry, Blenda always positive, trying to fix all confrontations and Waver getting into trouble with people and equipment. Carl and Walter always busy with equipment repairing and had formed a bond of friendship seldom seen with competing engineers on such long voyages. Their wives, Lovey and Zoe, also enjoyed a bonding that was very appropriate for them.

The young people tried hard to be of some use other than the Thespian kind. In their good intentions, they seemed to get in the way of running the ship. Porc Penn, Waver's close friend and Waver were the constant culprits in these mischievous events. The two sleep pods got little use because only Porc and Waver required the stasis resting but Battle was hesitant to put them in. Also Porc and Waver constantly thought others were getting privileges if they slept in the stasis pods, there-by passing them. Battle needed them to help keep his command on track.

They all had a special way of saying, "are we there yet?" This infuriated the old Counselor no end, to the extent, he sent several to the brig to keep their mouths shut. Bread and water was not much different that the fare the crew shared as they neared the unexplored planet. Everything was in short rations as well as tempers.

It was a welcome bit of news for the group as Carl informed the Counselor that they had reached a distance that could be scanned for life in the unchartered planet. The news circulated through the ship and brought a new voice of enthusiasm to all.

Carl and Battle hovered over the scanning displays looking for warm blood life in the yet far reaches of space yet to be traveled. They were still too far away to correctly analyze the displays on the screens. The formula to come off MacPherson's Arch and out of hyperspace, to cease mega hyper speed would take Carl and Walter awhile to correctly enter all the data configurations into the ship's computer to make a safe and sound landing on the new planet. That was all right because the landing was still days away.

The ship was filled with excitement as some scallywags were released from the brig, and Blenda and some of the other women were preparing some real food. Carl's wife Lovey was very good at making a stew out of the few fixings left in the larder. Zoe was Walter's wife who had a knack at making pastries from scratch that made the mouth water with anticipation. Donuts were the people's favorite.

The days followed with a kind of celebration atmosphere that seemed to soothe Battle Winslet. Getting this close to his goal was very satisfying to the old warrior. Blenda found Battle one day whistling to himself.

"What is the reason for your good humor, Battle?"

"We are so close to the time when I can take my rightful place on this new habitable planet and of course; you will be my queen."

"This king idea won't go very far with these young free spirited people. I think you must reconsider your plans for that kind of dominance on the new planet. They are more prone to a democratic kind of government, that their forefathers had on earth." Blenda spoke the truth to the perturbation of the Counselor.

He might have to wait and win over his subjects to sovereign rule later, a little at a time, he thought. "Well, we will see if the Hope Merchant has formed any kind of government when we find them. If they have, we should just infuse ourselves into that form and change it gradually, like it was done on earth, as I win over all the subjects to my way of superior thinking."

Just like the frog that sat in a pan of cold water and was unable to hop out of the water when it was *slowly being heated,* thought Blenda. Blenda just knew trouble lay ahead as she thought of ways to side track this kind of troubling thinking. She knew that deep down Battle had some very admirable qualities that included occasional intelligent reasoning. She hoped she could find this attribute before any confrontations with Rusty Bolt and company. She had known about Rusty back on earth. He had been at the top of his class at the academy. His accomplishments were known by many in the space community as a well-balanced and gregarious individual. Blenda was aware that Rusty had distinguished himself in the sciences as well as the arts. A young man with a great future in the space realm as well as an instigator of new and bright innovations for colonizing.

All of these facts in Blenda's mind gave her the shivers when she envisioned that they would have to counter the persona of Battle Winslet. Blenda's real concern was about her daughter, Whisper. This girl had been the one bright star in the life of Blenda. A girl with beauty and brains. A hope for the Winslet's that was never spoken of except by Blenda to Whisper. Blenda hadn't lasted this long for no reason. She would put her head down and meet the unexpected difficulties with that rare talent mothers seem to have. To overcome all adversaries at any cost, was a mother's instinct, to protect her children like a tigress that knows no boundaries. Just as Blenda made these confirmations in her will and started to form a plan for victory, a shout was heard from the bridge.

"What happened to the scanning equipment? Where are the indicators of the new planet? I can't see any thing in the scanners. The sensors are all down."

The big booming voice of Battle was all that was needed for Carl and Walter to come running up to the bridge for a lesson in competence and indulgent behavior.

CHAPTER TWENTY FIVE

Rusty and his group made it back to the ship where Whisper and Sparks as well as Rexanne Wheeler, Sparks and Rod had been waiting and praying the group to return. They had been trying to use all the scanning equipment with infrared capabilities to search for the missing crew. Because they were underground, the ships remaining crew was never were able to receive any positive signals. They even used Pep for some scouting about, but he took them only to a large boulder with a gaping hole and there the search ended.

As the Hope Merchant's crew settled in for a renewed effort to locate a suitable site for colonization, a communal buzz was the event of the day. All of the events concerning the Root people and Leggs were relayed to those that had not gone underground. The time went very fast as the little band packed up, and set sail for new regions in their ship that was getting low on fuel for any extensive reconnoitering. Leaving an area that was slightly familiar was justly difficult.

Searching the planet was an interesting procedure. Every one was excited as to the place they would locate. The temperate land was very beautiful and bucolic. The southern hemisphere was still a torrent of extremes, with many volcanoes and thermal vents. Geysers were everywhere, and deserts were common. Even a vast rain forest was noted in the equatorial regions. The northern hemisphere soon was the only center of interest to the group. They again located near fresh water in the form of a river. Close by was the larger body of water that was certainly an ocean of sorts. The rolling hills seemed so fertile and inviting for crops and clearings for habitation. Foothills were close by and a range of mountains was situated in the distance. The land appeared to be an immense plateau. The air was clean, and the trees present were mostly conifers with a few hardwoods indicating the remote chance of intruding upon any possible habitat of Root people. When the site was chosen by an over whelming majority the group quickly settled in and began again the process of making a livable village.

It was soon after these events that it became quite evident that Midge was ready to give birth to the first child at the New Hope settlement. Dr. Rexanne Wheeler was prepared with her new clinic. Midge and Dirk had been preparing for this day for some time and with some trepidation. It was of a mild type, not knowing what the future held for the little band of explorers and colonizers.

Dirk and Midge had discussed all the options about a new birth on an unknown planet and had decided it was worth the risk. They had determined that fear would not dictate the reality of their hopes and dreams. They had seen too many friends and relatives avoid any new or adventuresome activity, thereby missing out on a life of excitement and intense interest. That was one of the reasons they had applied for this long and arduous trip of unknown destinies.

Dirk was thought to be a nerdy person but was in fact, a very interesting person of great intelligence. He was tall and owlish looking with oversize eyeglasses that belied his gentle but disciplined nature. He did not appear to belong to little plump Midge, but their marriage was very complete and healthy. Dirk was always ready to add to any discussion if asked. His input was always welcome and very informative to anyone that inquired. Dirk had a sense of humor if you could find it. Little snippets such as when the Root people were discovered, he quipped, "that it was nice that we dug up such a cooperative tribe of humanoids." A kind of comment usually ascribed to Joel. Even when describing Midge in her last month of pregnancy Dirk offered up this observation. "Midge is not as big as a barn but she could outsize a small house they knew about."

These quips even outdid Joel's comment. "Midge is like spring that is busting out all over." All in good fun.

Dirk was the epitome of an expectant father as he brought his little wife to the colony's clinic where Dr. Wheeler was ready and waiting, having been notified of the pending event, earlier. Water broke and contractions were coming quite regularly. The time was in the middle of the night as usual. Dirk,being so nervous and excited he was ushered out of the clinic after Midge had gone back to resting, and he began to pace about the door trying to listen for any telltale signs of new life and his wife's shouts of joy. He was soon joined by some of the band of colonizers, in the early morning, giving him encouraging words of confidence and assurance. All of the group began to pace with Dirk as the hours began to pile up with only occasional noises of dubious origins were heard with trepidation.

Each member of the group tried to analyze the powerful sounds with little effect on Dirk. He was certain that all was going just fine and his ears were not the only source for his conviction. He and Midge had prayed many times about this impending birth and were given assurances that the procedure would be just fine. Dirk finally gave out his assessment of the situation, "after all, wasn't Dr. Wheeler the finest surgeon on the planet?"

Every one gave out a hearty guffaw.

Everyone also gave a warm smile as the tension was cut down to size. It was several hours later that the shouts of joy and a tiny, but firm and lusty cry of a newborn was heard. The new father rushed into the clinic to welcome his son and Midge into his adoring arms. Rexanne had a time to keep the scene controlled and calm as all were crying and laughing at the same time. All the members of the colony heard the good news and came as one to congratulate the new parents and the newest member of New Hope. The boy was named Noel because he was the first gift born on New Hope. Midge and Dirk met at Christmas and were married one year later on Christmas Their bouncing baby boy would be a reminder of the great importance of Christmas. It was also determined that Christmas was at home.

Noel Dare was baptized into the new colony be a screeching or whining sound of high mechanical proportions that indicted a Comet Chaser in trouble. Looking up the assembled group became aware of a Comet Chaser flying overhead in an erratic way that meant it was out of control. In only seconds, the ship vanished over the horizon to its unknown destiny. It was agreed that in that condition it would have to make a crash landing somewhere over the high hills it had just passed because the mountains lay ahead, quite high.

The band agreed that a search party would have to venture into the hills and the area beyond to see if any one would have survived. In the old fashion way, on foot. The freighter was low on rocket fuel so that any possible extended flight was dismissed. They all agreed that they should not use the ship for any flights in case the ship was needed to be involved for any known emergencies. Some thought the ship should be disassembled for reasons of resoluteness in the determination of staying here on New Hope, just like the colonizers of old.

Rusty had Sparks to contact Bert Bright and advise him of the situation and their plan for search and rescue. The search party was made up of Joel, Gloria, Evie, and Rod. These four could travel fast and keep the home base advised of their progress. Pep acted as though he would like to go also, but Whisper would not let him.

In the meantime, Whisper had taken over the care and duty of Noel and his mother. Midge was glad, as was Dirk for all the help. Dirk was kept busy making some more furniture and enlarging the Dare's hut for the new arrival. In fact, everyone was busy and excited about all of the new circumstances.

The search party was equipped and sent out early in the morning with supplies and equipment for several days searching. Rexanne had wanted to go but Rusty thought it best for her to stay with Midge and Noel. The search group would take basic medical supplies to administer first aid, if needed.

Sparks had contacted Bert Bright and had given him the exact coordinates that Comet Chaser One was observed in its last heading. Rusty stayed at base to help in anyway he could when needed by either group. Rusty was trying to go over in his head, all of the possibilities that might occur with this Chaser so close to his chosen area for initial habitation. If Battle Winslet was on board and alive it would bode poorly for those that did not want to live under his monarchy. Rusty knew of the man's desire to be a king in a new environment. His daughter had confirmed this notion more that once. The planet was so large and pristine no one needs to lord it over anyone else. The problem back on earth was that people were stumbling over each other causing constant friction and quarreling let alone massive contaminations and toxic conditions. For some reason they were also multiplying like rabbits.

Rusty thought if Battle wanted to be King, he could take his group away from here and start a monarchy in another far off location. Rusty's group would have no part of that monarchy business and was already drafting a code of ethics and a constitution to live by. There would be no confrontation if it was left up to Rusty and his group, but they would be prepared to fight if need be to keep their freedom and way of life. They had come too far to be intimidated or harassed by some bygone warrior of a dying order. Rusty made contact with his investigating group of four just as they had reached the top of the hills.

"Can you see any smoke or signs of a crash?"

Joel answered, " No sign of any kind of that nature. We do see some interesting geological formations hidden down the other side of the hills. It almost looks like ruins of an orderly nature. Rod is so excited he has started to run down the hill in great anticipation but of little wariness. I will try to get him to slow down so that we can all arrive at this area together. We don't need any more dangerous surprises; Joel out."

Rusty put up the COM unit as he noticed Whisper caring for little Noel in a loving fashion that surprised the Captain. She brought the infant over to let Rusty have a look at the lusty little boy. Her comment gave Rusty a jolt.

"Isn't he sweet? I was wondering if the Comet Chaser Two might come back after their search and spend some time with us. I would think Bert Bright would still be the leader of that expedition, don't you?"

Rusty agreed with her as he thought about how babies sometimes brought out the mother in young girls. Young girls that needed to meet young boys for possible courting. The day was looking brighter for Rusty's group and the future of New Hope.

CHAPTER TWENTY SIX

Joel tried to call back Rod Wheeler as the Archeologist moved down the hill in great haste and with little caution in a new and unknown region. It was understandable since Rod had noticed the area below could be ruins of a bygone civilization. This was one of the reasons he had been chosen to be a crew member on this unique voyage. Joel saw that Rod had disappeared into a dense growth of vegetation and faintly heard the archeologists loud shouts of joy and excitement. The group proceeded with caution when entering the dense brushy vegetation. A good place for an ambush. The cries of discovery from Rod scared off any of the smaller animals they had seen scattered in all directions only minutes before. When the three came out of the brush and entered a clearing they saw Rod on his hands and knees looking at the ground with Sherlock Holmes' intensity.

"There has been an advanced above ground society on this planet," verbalized Rod to no one in particular. He touched the stones and ground as he effused his observations out loud. His entire countenance was delirious with discovery and prolific observations. Only Joel's stern official voice brought Rod back to the problem at hand.

"Rod, we must leave and continue our search for the failing Comet Chaser we saw in trouble. It must come first, but we will certainly try to come here again to study the ruins and document the entire area."

"I know you are right, but I was so caught up in this unique discovery I was beside myself. Just look at the size of these stones the houses and walls are made. Let's get going over the next hill. Maybe we will see more evidence of humanoid habitation."

Moving forward, the group of four had advanced to the next higher hill and saw only great flat grasslands with various kinds of herding animals that scattered as they noticed the intruders. Many looked like deer or antelope and ran like the wind. Others were similar to our bison and loped or stood their ground, fearing nothing. It was quite apparent that a food supply of meat would be sufficient to feed the little colony for some time, until their domesticated animals began to multiply.

Looking all around with the elecnoculars, Joel was still unable to locate the faltering flying Comet Chaser. The landscape seemed to go on forever with hills and dales until the mountain range melded with them in the distance. These indications gave Joel the hint that the planet was larger than earth.

The craft could have crashed or landed in one of many dips or dales in the landscape. To continue, the group settled on a time factor of two days searching and then turn back if no contact was made with the distressed ship. The group made about ten kilometers so far because of the agreeable surface. The streams were small and the vegetation in clumps so that traveling was uncomplicated.

Rod was sad about leaving his new found ruins and what it might mean to science in general and the searchers in particular. His comments were of a positive nature. "I'll bet we find some more ruins on this part of the planet. It is so correct for habitation. Everyone keep your eyes alert for any more signs of habitation by our new planet people."

The group of four moved forward in a fanned out position so that more area could be investigated as well as a form of possible protection from unseen adversaries. Joel, Gloria, Rod and Evie made a competent group by following the gradient and dips of the land so that one was always in sight on another.

The day was very pleasant with the temperature warm enough for no need for heavy clothing but cool enough so that no one was sweating. The wind came from what they had decided was the west with clouds big and white, lazily drifting across the expanse of sky before the mountains. The pinkish sun was hanging in the sky giving off warmth but not sultriness. If it wasn't for the seriousness of the search, the group could imagine themselves on a hike and picnic back home. But, this was not the case. The territory was unexplored and dangerous because of so many unknowns. The first day melted into evening with nothing new to report back to Rusty. On a small grassy knoll it was declared to be the end of day one, and a campsite was made.

Three tents were set in a crescent, a fire and food soon completed the camp. Soon the little group of searchers were asleep with only one set on guard while the others slept. Gloria had volunteered to be first, as it was agreed that shift would be well suited for one so animated of the four. She had set a folding chair on the highest part of the knoll to have the advantage of height for surveying the surrounding landscape. Gloria was a hardy soul with stamina and energy to spare for a person of medium stature. As the hour moved towards midnight by her watch, she fought the heaviness of her eyelids but lost the battle near the end of her watch.

A heavy but kindly hand placed on her shoulder accompanied by words of enquiry brought her back to the highest state of alertness.

"What do you see on the far hill or are my eyes playing tricks on me?"

Evie stood by her side with her elecnoculars trying determine if a light was seen on the far horizon. When Gloria took the elecnoculars to give her impression of the area, she came up with a negative.

"I can see no light or even a glow. It must have been a star or planet appearing on the horizon for a moment."

Evie suggested Gloria to go to bed as she would now take up the guard duty for the next shift. A solid embrace of the women sent the two to their respective places as Evie felt for her weapon and to be sure it was at the ready.

As Evie settled in, she kept scanning the area, she thought she had seen the light. It was close to the end of her shift when the area that Evie scanned gave off a glow. The area was about ten kilometers in the distance according to her scan. The glow remained for at least five minutes but when she decided to wake Joel the glow had disappeared. She told Joel of the far off glow and to keep an eye open for it might mean some other strange sightings. Joel had decided to let the others sleep for the following day could be quite arduous. He went back to his tent as Rod took the last watch.

Joel tried to sleep, but it was only in spurts and fits that sleep came to him. Gloria tried to tell him to relax, and the day would bring a fresh start as well as a new outlook on their situation. His thoughts still ranged over the many possibilities that lay ahead.

Maybe the glow was a signal fire or even worse it might be the Comet Chaser on fire. It might be some natural phenomena of this area, like swamp gas. Maybe a new and unknown group of humanoids were trying to lure the group further into dangerous territory. It was a quandary that moved about Joel's brain until sweats and first light brought him up out of his fitful slumber.

Rod had just returned to his sleeping bag and Joel was on the last watch. With the sky becoming lighter by the minute no far off glow could be seen even if it was there. Sensing no further sightings, Joel came back to camp and began the duty of preparing breakfast as quietly as possible, but soon Gloria was up and assumed that duty as she was desirous to do.

When breakfast was finished the four sat around and discussed the events and possible sighting in the far western horizon. All possibilities were discussed as well as plans for the day. It was decided to advance in the direction of the glow in a slightly circular route to come upon any activity on its flank.

Rod had the com-unit and was directed to contact Rusty at base camp and divulge all that had happened during the night here on the knoll. Rod also told of their plan for the day and asked if Rusty had any suggestions that might benefit the search. Rusty only reiterated that the area was unknown and to be careful. The lay of the and as well as vegetation or animals were not to be trusted as earth-like.

"Be careful as foxes, as you are all indispensable to colonizing this planet," were his parting words of caution and wisdom.

Packing up the camp gear the four headed down the knoll for regions unknown. Taking bearings before they left, Joel headed off to the right in a slightly flanking of their earlier glow sighting. Joel felt like he was totally responsible for the group and turned over in his head all kinds of cautionary activity. He calculated in his head the amount of food and water that would be needed for the trip in and a return trip. Could they trust any water found on this expanse of land? Did they have enough ammunition if needed for any confrontation.? If the glow was a Comet Chaser crash did they have the expertise to administer any medical treatments? If Battle were alive did he still hold a lethal grudge against Rusty and the Hope merchant crew? The questions seemed to have no end in Joel's mind, but it made the time pass quickly.

Rod went to his knees as he found some sign of humanoid habitation on the track they were on." It appears someone has been in this area recently. These tracts indicate some had foot gear and some were barefoot.

CHAPTER TWENTY-SEVEN

Rusty was busy with the rest of the group of colonizers. He kept the camp apprised of all of Joel's group's activities. Dr.Wheeler was busy with the new baby and Noel's mother. It was determined that Midge hadn't enough milk for the bustling baby child. Rexanne was trying to concoct a formula that would suffice the requirements for Noel. Whisper was a tireless assistant in this endeavor. Whisper had even volunteered to scout out around in case an animal of goat-like or cow-like attributes could be found out in the countryside with milk a possibility. Rusty countermanded the suggestion with the comment, "no one should leave camp alone, for any reason."

Even with Pep at her side all the time, Rusty felt that a foray into the surrounding hills and dales should only be taken when several members were free from camp responsibilities. Whisper was convinced that Rusty was correct in his assessment of the situation but still ambled further and further from camp on her many forays.

Eryka kept busy devising skits for the evening's entertainment while Dirk helped in the formulation of a milk substitute. Whisper was busy making food suggestions and cooking for the hungry group. Midge was getting to be quite plumpish and Rexanne had put her on a diet. . Whisper started a small garden as well as locating berries and fruit in the surrounding area. After making positive as to the acceptability of the food items, she introduced them to the camp as suitable and tasty. All of these endeavors Whisper accomplished without any fanfare. She ate small potions to be certain of no side effects or toxicity when asked how she knew that to be true she confessed to her imprudent actions. She was of course, gently chastised for her activity, and advised that Dirk should go with her on any future forays outside the camp's perimeter, advising her to not taste everything found.

Rusty was wrestling with the thought of taking the freighter up for a quick scan to locate the possible wreckage of the sputtering Comet Chaser One. Rusty had contacted Bert Bright for his advice on the subject. Bert had settled in an area far from Rusty and his group and his Comet Chaser was practically out of fuel for any non-targeted flights. Bert wondered why Rusty had not used the air car on the freighter. Rusty had to reply that it was all in pieces, disassembled and still in its crate. It would take several days to uncrate it and the to assemble it with the few experienced crew hands to accomplish the job. If the group decided to try another location to finally settle in, the uncrated air car would become a liability in trying to re-stow the partially assembled unit. Bert ending by relating his offer to help in anyway possible. "Just give me a buzz on the com-link and I will use the remaining Comet fuel to come to your aid. That may cause unique problems, but we will come."

Rusty gave his offer of help too. Rusty kept in constant contact with Joel as he had related about the glow on the horizon and related all the possibilities it might mean. This gave Rusty the inner signal of danger. That gut feeling that came to him from time to time. The only thing left for Rusty to do was to pray his little investigating group of four was ever vigilant and constantly on guard.

Noel wasn't doing well on his meager supply of milk with the new formula concocted by Rexanne and Dirk. The little fellow was losing weight and began to take on a gray pallor. Whisper was so upset that she demanded that Rusty allow her and Dirk go on the prowl for any animal life that could be of assistance to supply Noel with sustenance. "A little mother's milk and rice broth was not enough for the growing infant," said Whisper with waving arms of emphasis. After Rusty had exhausted all of the reasons that the search probably wouldn't produce any results he relented and gave the two a one day permit to look for anything of a consequence of help for Midge and Noel.

On the next day, the two set out to scout for any animal of the bovine species. They had seen several herds of grazing animals that might fill the bill; some looked like goats. Dirk carried most of the supplies as Whisper and Pep moved ahead at a fast clip. Dirk had a stun gun to use if needed, as it most probably would be. Whisper seemed to have an aversion to guns but implied that she would use one if needed to bring to Noel needed milk or it's equivalent.

As soon as Whisper topped one hill, her dog Pep, would race to the next hill and wait for the duo. With this kind of advancements, the trio reached distant lands in a hurry. Pep appeared to sense or know why the exercise was being conducted and waited patiently giving every indication of seeing nothing. This went on for more hills than Dirk wanted to climb but finally on one hill Pep waited in an anxious manner with wagging tail and muted sounds of success. Whisper purchased the brow of the hill in a cautious and stealthy manner. Below her and Pep was a herd of cow-like animals browsing lazily in the afternoon warmth. No breezes gave away the scent of two humans and a dog. When Dirk finally reached the top, he was delighted to see the herd, as well as a chance to lie down and rest a moment. Whisper could see several of the cows with calves and wanted Dirk to hurry up and set the stun gun to target one of the mother cows if that was what they were. Shaggy dark coats with great hindquarters gave them an appearance of Bison Bovines, but nothing like any earth bound creatures. Dirk tried to talk Whisper into letting him kill one of the beasties for food. She pointed out that he should only stun one mother cow with calf, and then he could kill a lone bull. The calf must not be deprived of nourishment.

Dirk aimed the gun and set it on stun as he used his laser for sighting. One zap put the cow down and then Dirk set the gun on kill after sighting a young, horned bull before the herd noticed any disturbances and made his shot. This zap was louder than he realized and set the herd to moving. All but the cow and the bull moved away with the calf standing expectantly by the mother cow. Pep kept the calf at a safe distance as it bawled. Dirk and Whisper moved forward cautiously with Pep as a guard. The plan was to get the cow to give milk with Whisper's endeavors. Dirk would butcher as much of the bull as he could carry and then they would leave with haste before the herd came back for some saving antics for their downed members. Just as the two were finishing, Pep gave a warning signal because the herd was moving back to its original position for what purpose our threesome was not certain. With all they could carry, they moved out back up the hill and down the other side with nothing following them that they could detect. Pep again took the lead with many glances back for any sign of herd mentality for reprisal.

After about three hills, they slowed to a pace that allowed them to catch their breath and regain some stamina for the trek home. Whisper's canister of fresh milk was quite heavy for a young girl, but she refused any help that Dirk offered. Dirk was also very burdened with the meat on his back, but they knew this task was for comrades back at camp.

"I think we did real good," said Dirk as he caught his breath in short gasps.

Whisper agreed, as she held up the container of fresh milk for a little child that needed more nourishment.

"How lucky we were, but we'll have to do something like this every few days?" Dirk didn't answer right away for he already knew that this one foray was not the answer for the dilemma for Noel.

With a degree of awkwardness, Dirk gave Whisper a positive reply. "I hope that with this milk, Rexanne can use it to extend any formula to last many days. Then we won't have to come out too often to find a herd and repeat this operation. Maybe we will have to capture one of the mother beasts to afford a constant supply of milk. The group will certainly enjoy the meat we are bringing back, so I would say the entire day was a huge success."

Whisper gave the final thought on the subject. "I agree that next time we will have to bring back a cow and its calf if all goes well with this milk."

Pep gave a hearty bark to give his endorsement as he closely followed behind Dirk and his aromatic meat of the day

CHAPTER TWENTY-EIGHT

Rod was trying to see if the tracks were of the crew of Comet Chaser One. "The shoe prints are absolutely the kind issued to flight crews so it must be our lost Comet Chaser crew. The other barefoot prints are of the same design as our own but larger and adaptive to accommodate barefoot travel. I fear that our humans have fallen into the hands of natives of this region and probably taken as prisoners as we were awhile back. Rod talked to Joel through cupped hands, a little ways off to Joel's right."

"I pity the natives," said Joel with remembered justifiable aspersions. Joel also was listening intently, trying to formulate a plan that was not dangerous and not timid as well. "The first thing to do is to contact Rusty and give him our position and relate our findings here. We will tell him we think we must follow the tracks instead of looking for the spacecraft. Then we will follow Rusty's suggestion and listen to his reasoning," said Joel with hands cupped voice directed to Rod.

Gloria and Evie were close by on Joel's left as earlier suggested.

A disciplined crew would take this procedure. The four agreed as Rod contacted their base. Quite a long conversation followed with Joel and Rod each relating the happenings at their part of the group's situations. It was impossible to give Rusty an accurate location because no GPS was available on this planet at this time. After the lengthy discourse Joel told his group all that was said and that they would carefully follow the tracks but to take no action unless it was absolutely necessary. Essentially, we are to locate the possible captured crew and assess the situation for future action. Joel was told of Noel's situation and that Dirk and Whisper were trying to remedy the situation and were absent from the base, searching for goats or bovines that give milk.

Rod had made a thorough examination of the tracks and gave his report as fellows:

"I see about six different shoe marks and maybe ten various or different foot prints. I also have detected some blood droplets so one or more persons must wounded. There is no indication of anyone on a stretcher, but the blood droplets are constant and large. We need to travel in that direction to follow the group."

Pointing towards what appeared to be a horizon without an end, they began an upward trek. When they attained the top of a rise, it revealed a great body of water. It could very well be an ocean or a massive lake. With stealth as their directive, the group of four lay on their bellies to scope out the area. It wasn't difficult to see a group of people sitting or trussed up about the water guarded by a cadre of natives. Off in the distance horizon Gloria spotted a ship with a giant sail making its way towards the shore. The four watched with intent breath as the ship came close to shore and put a smaller craft in the water to land on the beach.

Evie was certain the humans below were in great danger. "We will have to try some sort of rescue for our human friends. The natives appear agitated and threatening."

Using his elecnoculars, Joel made out eight human Chaser Two crewmembers being guarded by at least four warrior types. The small watercraft landed and produced four more tribal types but having a regal bearing. What happened next was hard to understand. Much arguing and hand waving with shouts that could be heard by the four on their bellies. This went on for about an hour when some were sent to gather wood in the adjacent shore and to set a fire. Driftwood was gathered and large posts were set into the sandy beach as eight pillars. Each post evidently, to be the holding place for eight individual humans. Several women were also present in that trussed up condition. The women did not escape the threats and menacing gestures

The native humanoids continued to argue and make gestures of intimidating proportions. They jumped into the water and splashed water on their captives on occasion. It would have been comical if it had not been so threatening. One tall and regal person stood back and only observed as he went to each trussed up human and looked into their faces for any sign of fear after throwing water in their faces. At least that is what Joel thought. The warriors sat down at last and took time to eat and drink sustenance brought from the beached boat. At this juncture, the tall regal person addressed the entire group with much fanfare accompanied by gestures towards the sky and sea. The day wore on like a great tire deflating as the sun was lowering on the westerly horizon.

Without any explanation, the captors all got into the beached boat and made for the larger ship at anchor off shore. Even with this turn of events, our people were still securely tied to their posts. The humanoids continued to make threatening gestures at their captives, threw spears, and shot arrows at the eight even from a watery distance. The Comet crew deftly avoided any direct hits from the projectiles, but the scene was one of lethal possibilities. As twilight seeped over the scene, the great ship sailed off and over the horizon out of sight.

This gave Joel and his band the opportunity to go down and free their fellow humans. Even with the knowledge of the captors having left the area, Joel's group moved down with great caution. As they neared the shore, they heard much cursing and oaths emanating from no other than Battle Winslet. When they made themselves known, Battle began to give commands and directives. Joel had his people release the seven others leaving Battle for last. This brought forth threats and anger of colossal proportions. Joel very carefully and with lowered voice told Battle, "You are not in control here and now, so just control your self and be thankful for the providence exhibited here this day. After Battle settled down, Joel had Battle untied with promises of cooperation from the old warrior.

"Freed by an underling at that," murmured Battle as his new situation became crystal clear.

Joel learned that the natives took this group because all the others in the Comet Chaser were unconscious, or appearing dead at the crash site.

When order was restored, the band of explorers provided each other with news of what was happening as well as guesses why their captors left without killing them. Battle told about the crippled ship and its crash landing. A list of causalities was produced as Gloria and Evie tended to the minor wounds and trauma of some of the eight survivors. The only thing left to do was to begin the journey back to the Comet Chaser's crash site.

The survivors here consisted of: Blenda and Battle Winslet, Bonnie Gale and Victor, Walter and Zoe, Carl and Lovey. The others are presumed dead or mortally wounded as the captors left them behind.

Blenda was pleased to hear of Whispers happiness in her new environment. Battle asked a lot of questions about Rusty and was of course, glad to hear of Bert Bright's safe landing. "It will be good to reunite with Chaser Two and Bertram," the old warrior mused. Battle seemed unusually mild mannered as he extracted everything about the new Hope settlement. Joel finally got the impression that Battle was not interested in the state of affairs at New Hope but was trying to have revealed to him any weaknesses in relationships. Truth was one of the first casualties of conflicts.

Joel then began his own enquiries about Battle and his survivor's plans for the days ahead. It was a game of thrust and parry, each not knowing if truth remained unadulterated. They would have to stop and make camp in the dark, as the party was very tired and weary. Joel selected a small valley with trees and a stream. A place where a fire could be set and hot food prepared.

Gloria made herself busy as any good cook would want to be with mouths to feed. Hot tea and coffee made the rounds. A hearty but thin soup gave everyone a feeling of being satisfied. Canned biscuits and dried fruit made up the balance because the supplies were limited. It seemed to be enough, as some provisions would have to be saved for breakfast. The fire was still cozy as many sleepy heads found a place to settle down. Joel directed Gloria to take the first watch and Rod could take the second. Evie and Joel would take the last two watches as the little party regained their strength and stamina.

Battle's group had stayed with Joel's at this point. Joel told his watchers to keep a special eye on Battle because the old warhorse was strangely quiet and mild mannered. The night passed uneventfully with only some snoring and groans of pain from a few wounded persons disturbing the peaceful night air.

When the morning came, Joel contacted Rusty on the com-link and suggested this group return to the crash site to see if any survivors existed. Rusty agreed and cautioned Joel not to split the group up when they moved towards the crash site with great caution.

"Take your time and try to ration supplies as well as allowing the people to recuperate so they could be helpful in carrying any saved supplies from the ship back to our base camp," Rusty advised as he signed off.

Joel had Evie and Rod go around the camp and ascertain each ones condition as food was served up by Gloria. "Determine if there are any dissents about going to the crash site to help any survivors.

It short order came the answer, "no one was against going back," reported Evie.

Joel received the report with relief as his team related that all were willing to return to the Comet Chaser One's crash site as soon as it was convenient. Even Battle was in hearty agreement since his son, Waver, might still be among the survivors.

In the morning, Rod and Battle were sent out as a point for the band of humans to make sure that no other planet people were not trying to scavenge or salvage anything from the crashed Comet Chaser.

The two point men keep up a lively pace and reached the crash site long before the rest of the group. When Joel and the others came upon the scene, Battle and Rod had effectively pulled out most of the injured passengers. Most were alive but in a dazed and traumatic condition.

Garner and Fairly Trapp along with another couple were placed on makeshift stretchers. Waver and his friend, Porc were also alive but bloodied. The two point men had set up a triage system where the more serious were close to the crash site in the shade and the lesser wounded were placed out of that area near some trees. Blenda treated Waver and his friend, Master Porc. Gloria and Evie continued to minister to the others as Battle tried to give orders to all involved. This gesture was seen to dilute the authority of Joel. Joel countermanded several of the bellowings as he felt his stun gun in a fashion that caught Battle's eye. After this motion all was returned to a serenity as some of the men prepared to bury the dead not far from the crash site. Joel had Rod report back to Rusty as some of the others began to salvage all of the food and equipment that could be carried by a disadvantaged crew. It was a sad and painful day, but the activity had to be accomplished. The ship might be repaired or salvaged later.

When everything had been accomplished, Joel decided to camp for the night at a place distant from the crash sites in case any humanoids returned seeking booty. The group moved out with packs and bundles carried by everyone, including the women. Battle carried very little as Blenda chastised her husband.

About two kilometers a way from the crash site, Joel found a suitable place to stop. The trek was a good test to determine if all the acquisitions could be carried, without too much strain. No one complained as a fire was set, and food was prepared. More now that the crashed Comet's foodstuff had been retrieved. After eating, many sat about the fire discussing the recent events.

Battle with great gusto began to tell of the encounters with the big and brash natives.

"There were just too many of them for me as I was incapacitated to ward them off. They are taller than most of us with great feet and hands that are webbed. They have flat foreheads and curly dark hair covering much of their head and body. They have large, dark and piercing eyes that blink often. Their noses are large as are their mouths giving off high-pitched sounds and clicks. They are sea people if ever I saw any. If any of you noticed, everyone of them dipped themselves into the water from time to time splashing us to see if that helped or hindered us."

Joel said to himself, "first it was root people and now sea people, where could humans colonize without upsetting a planet of beings already living in this huge untamed world?"

CHAPTER TWENTY-NINE

Rexanne and Midge were waiting for Whisper and Dirk. When the two came over the last hill with the welcoming barks of Pep, the base camp was delighted for their safe return. Dirk had been so caught up in his activities he had failed to report to Rusty. Rusty was not too concerned and wanted to wait for nightfall before interrupting any revelations about prey by Dirk or Whisper.

The captured milk was given to Rexanne for study and irradiation to preserve it for many days. Rexanne would also separate all the milk's components to try to duplicate mother's milk. She would then reconstitute a fluid and fortify it with the bovine milk. With irradiation, a large volume could be kept for a long period without spoilage. A complicated and time-consuming exercise but imperative for the health and well being of Noel. Whisper was congratulated for her retrieving the milk and not spilling it on the way back to camp. Roxanne's comment was met with an eagerness by Whisper. "If we can get this human milk duplicated, you and Dirk will have to go back and bring back a cow and calf for a continuous supply of milk." Whisper loved challenges and adventures into the unknown.

Eryka was helping Rexanne with all of the complicated physiology procedures to the dismay of Whisper. She liked to help in these procedures. Whisper was glad that her family survived the crash but knew everything would change when they were reunited here at base camp. To keep busy she and Pep tried their hand at chicken and animal husbandry and attempted to make a garden to test some of the seeds that had been carried aboard the freighter for a year. A few animals had been allowed to reproduce, and Whisper cared for the progeny. It would become apparent that a permanent site would have to be chosen soon. The space was limited on the Hope Merchant spacecraft as a depot of the varied and complex equipment. Everyone kept busy with daily chores and let down their surveillance of the surroundings except for Pep.

The dog made many forays into the landscape from time to time. One day Pep would bring back a rabbit-like creature and the next day it might be another animal that could be called a ground hog. Some of these were used as food while others were discarded as unsuitable. One time a bird was brought to the feet of Whisper who received it with much fanfare because it was a perfect looking fowl that looked like a prairie chicken or a domestic chicken. It was prepared and eaten with great satisfaction by all, for this kind of bird would supplement their food supply, which was beginning to get low. Pep was rewarded mightily giving him the impetus to bring back one almost everyday. The area was filled with an abundant supply of food according to Pep.

Rusty in due course received Joel's communication that the survivors would be coming in that evening. The group was tired and very hungry as little food was prepared by the group, too eager to get to Rusty's campsite. They also restated the need for Rexanne to be prepared for some minor surgery. Joel also asked that several of Rusty's people be dispatched over the hills in a westerly direction to help carry some of the salvaged stuff because the wounded could hardly carry it another step. Rusty answered in the affirmative and sent Sparks and Whisper. The family reunion would take place on the hills with Pep in attendance initiating the possibility of another prairie bird on the group's return. Sparks and Whisper started almost immediately after finding some equipment that would help carry items; some snack food and first aid supplies. The twosome began to climb the westerly hill with much anticipation.

After about two hours, the two groups met and celebrated with hugs and barks of joy. Blenda and Whisper especially took time to embrace and to discuss about happenings as mother and daughter might. Battle just seemed to mumble greetings to the rescuers as Waver and his friend Porc appeared bored as they stood back from the rest of the group. Porc had lost both of his parents in the crash and that would explain his vacant countenance. Waver had no such excuse for his dour expression at all the joy and mini celebration.

Joel allowed the party to continue as the wounded rested and were given first aid by Whisper and Sparks. Food was distributed, and it seemed to refresh everyone, especially when told that the base camp was only a few hours away. Pep made the rounds with kisses and lickings for all the assemblage. The dog then went off into the surrounding area to hunt or scout. Soon he had returned with a nice fat bird that was immediately prepared on the spot for all to enjoy. This seemed to revive everyone to Spark's and Whisper's satisfaction. Eventually, when the day was beginning to wane into an afternoon, Sparks and Whisper shared in the transport of much of the salvage, by dragging supplies between two poles brought by them, allowing the rest to take it easy. The group moved out with great expectations of rest and recuperation that lay ahead. Battle took the lead to impress everyone with his stamina and fortitude. He apparently also wanted to demonstrate that he was still the leader of this expedition. Just as night was falling all about, they reached Rusty's campsite. The reunited band of humans was given complete treatment with the wounded attended by Dr. Wheeler including some minor surgery. In the meantime, Rusty had contacted Lambert Bright at his location. Lambert was excited about happenings at that end. He was amazed that so many survived the Comet's crash. He asked Rusty to give battle his regards and awaited any new directives. Rusty reminded Bert he was now his own man having piloted a spacecraft for a year. In addition, that Battle and Bert were no longer in any governmental service requiring a chain of command or subservience on Bert's part. Bert received this bit of enlightenment with a real sense of relief.

Bert began to relate that his group had made friends with a band of indigenous people that looked and acted just like earthlings of old.

"They have many tools. Some of the metal is iron with silver and gold in ceremonial abundance. They also have domesticated a variety of animals for work and food. They have befriended our group with a semblance of friendliness that made us feel as though they were welcoming an old lost tribe of the planet. This tribal colony is large and comfortable situated close to a mountain range close to one of the planets oceans and several large rivers. We are learning the language and are easily melding into the tribe's daily activities. The area is large and would support your group if you wanted to come and settle here."

Rusty was at first dumbfounded by this encouraging news. It was almost too good to be true. *Indigenous peoples so much like friendly, and us humans* thought the young man. A myriad of possibilities ran through Rusty's head as he visualized the colonization of the planet in the years and generations to come. Now all he had to do was to convince his entourage that the move would be in the best interests of the lasting colonization for the planet. Sounding a clarion call he had the people assemble for the news that Bert had recently transmitted.

The group received the news with a variety of responses in the ensuing discussions. Battle wanted his group to follow him into the interior for his permanent colony. This was acceptable to Rusty and his people for they had mentioned that a constitution and bill of rights was next on the menu here at Rusty's settlement. This caused Battle to frown and state, "that kind of stuff would not work at this level of colonizing for his group." Battle gave his view in a deep but winy voice, "So I would like a few supplies and a chance for us to migrate into the planet's interior.

"This small group needs a definite and powerful kind of government to survive in these circumstances," continued Battle with Waver and Porc agreeing with nods of their heads. Only Blenda of that group had doubts in her eyes as she lovingly looked at Whisper and her blossoming womanhood.

"When we go," said battle with finality in his voice, "we will need a varied supply of goods to last us a long time, especially if your bunch are retreating to a place of comfort and known circumstances"

"Remember Jamestown," added Joel to the assemblage.

Rusty had remembered Jamestown and had warned Bert to be ever vigilant. It appeared Battle had made up his group's mind and was preparing a list with directives to fetch supplies to meet his needs. At which point Rusty pulled the old counselor to one side and in very precise words told him that nothing was going to leave the freighter without Rusty's or Joel's approval. Battle replied with murmured blue acquiesces.

The next few days were filled with stresses and strains as Battle's band made off with supplies in abundance. They also wanted the only land car and asked that he be left behind so it could carry all the acquired booty with battle in tow. Rusty and Joel talked it over and finally gave in to Battle so he could carry all the supplies that had been pulled from the freighter. They also gave generators, carbon fuel, water purifiers, tools, rechargeable energy packs, food and much more. A supply that would be difficult to move in one trip even with the land car.

When all his people had recovered from the crash ordeal, they all assembled to bid farewell to Rusty and his followers. The scene was a mixture of joy and sadness. Others demanded that they would stay here with Rusty and company. Walter and Zoë wanted to stay but at the urging and cajoling by Battle ultimately went with him. Victor and wife Bonnie Gale made the decision to stay, all to the consternation of Battle since Blenda wanted to stay.

When Battle and his remaining group had left, Joel and Rusty decided to make some forays in the area for a spot unknown to Battle. That old warrior attracted difficulties like fleas to a dog. Clearing the base camp and packing up was done with little difficulty as the exercise had been repeated before. Whisper advised that they go towards the area she had found the cows.

Even Pep had a difficult time leaving the area. Rusty saw that his group was all aboard and then piloted the big freighter up and headed once more in a westerly direction, leaving the campsite looking clean and undisturbed, unconsciously moving in Bert's direction.

Rusty leaned over to his copilot, Joel, and declared, "this has got to be it for the fuel in our craft has just fallen to the lowest mark."

Joel answered, "it's do or die now, eh Cap?"

CHAPTER THIRTY

Bert was enjoying a time of relaxation with a comfortable chair beneath him and a cold beverage by his side. The air was gentle and pleasantly mild. The day's work and directives were completed as he watched his people mingle and meld with the indigenous group they had found. Actually, the tribe had found them trying to set up a settlement on this mountain plateau meadow.

Bert remembered how two individuals coming slowly towards his group with a raised tree branch approached them. It was certainly a sign of peace or halcyon demonstration. After introductions and much gesturing a type of informative discourse followed. They were a peace-loving nation of individuals that welcomed the lost brothers of the land. (Humans) Mawpics welcoming their brothers with open arms. Bert made peace with them by exchanging small gifts and sweet delicacies. A short time later, the two returned with their entire compliment of Mawpics. A band of about one hundred was soon settled around Bert and company with much ceremony and pomp. Dancing and a kind of singing made the event quite pleasant.

The following days were filled with sharing and constructing living quarters for the lost brothers and sisters. Bert was quite amazed at the similarities of the two people's activities. The Mawpics learned the earthling's language with a rapidity that was uncanny, as though they were made to be more earthly than anyone might have guessed.

Riley Striker and Bristle Fume caused trouble, as usual. A stockade was built to house any fractious persons; therefore, it was pointed out to the two that would be their home if they didn't leave the Mawpic ladies alone. This pestering by Riley and Bristle was causing some consternation among the Mawpics. Any apprehension on their part gave Bert and his people a wary disposition from this point on. Bert was glad that Rusty had told him to be ever vigilant when they last conversed before a planned rendezvous the following day.

The next day the big freighter came in on the coordinates Bert had given Rusty. It was away from the new settlement to allay any fears the Mawpics might have. The trip had taken Rusty et al over an entire continent at sub light speed. After landing with some fear and trepidation from the Mawpics, all soon became peaceful once again. Greetings from all around, and in due course Rusty told Bert of Battle's departure and planned kingdom. Bert was not surprised as he had an inkling of Battle's sense of colonization.

While the entire assemblage began unloading everything, essential for their new living arrangements, they all ostensibly realized the hard work ahead of them. At this juncture, they would have to carry or lug essentials and make more trips or bring the big ship closer when the Mawpics had been acclimated to its presence. The Comet Chaser was much smaller and had landed before the Mawpics had been introduced to the colonization activities.

The Hope Merchant must appear to them as a grand castle or temple.

It was natural for Whisper and Bert to gravitate together for light conversation of the inquiring kind. Pep was not to be denied as he made his presence felt by jumping and barking for attention. When all were loaded-up, Bert led the way back to the settlement and the Mawpic's welcome. It was not as joyous as Bert had hoped because the Mawpics were holding Riley Striker by the scruff of the neck with anger in their eyes. Riley had tried to lure a young Mawpic lady away from the camp. Even though unsuccessful Riley was apprehended and held for judgment according to the Mawpic's girl's father. The indigenous people had a council of five to govern the group, Rusty was told by Bert. This event would prove to be a real detriment to the settlement's building and progress. The Mawpics gestured they wanted to take Riley back to their area of the plateau for a judgment of the offense. Bert and Rusty tried to relate to the apparent father of the girl that their earthling brothers should try and judge the malefactor. But to no avail. The Mawpics were adamant that Riley goes with them for his judgment. Bert allowed the delegation to go with Rusty's benediction with a proviso that one of our people accompanied Riley as advocate or counsel. Bristle Fume volunteered but Bert would allow only Garner Trapp to go. Garner was smart and a large man in size. He also was well versed in articulating the Mawpics language and some customs recently learned. Fairly, Garner's wife was also sent to keep the feminine view in mind. A good strong woman of a virtuous nature is Fairly Trapp. Several others volunteered but this group was very capable, opined Bert. "I believe the meandering rascal will get a fair trial with our people in tow."

After the Mawpics had gone with their Earthling brothers, Rusty, Joel, Evie and Gloria with the others present began to select sites for their new village. The area was huge with accesses to flowing water, complete with fish. Large grassy fields available would accommodate the animals for grazing, some native species already in sight. Planting areas appeared everywhere. The valley below provided warm uplifting breezes in the daytime and the mountains above washed the plateau with cool breaths at night. The area was perfect, all agreed.

Rusty received a call from Battle telling of his group's settlement in a big valley. All was going smoothly he related in a deceptive sort of way, but they would need more fossil fuel, and foodstuff.

Battle wondered if one of them would fly the freighter back to his area for more supplies as they were running out of provisions.

"I am sorry we can't comply for we have situations of our own. Besides, you were told that the parting was of a permanent nature and you could take all the supplies you needed to establish a place of your own choosing. We even gave you the land car with enough fuel to last many months. What happened to it all?"

Battle answered in muted tones that indicted he had not been able to more effectively control his circumstances.

"Well when the car was fully assembled, Waver and Porc took some joy rides and in the process spilled a large quantity of fuel. They and some others also partied often, consuming large quantities of basic foodstuffs. I bawled them out and told them not to take the land car out unless I gave them permission, and to stop partying. I hoped they followed my orders, but you know, boys will be boys."

Rusty said that they could not come and Battle would have to work things out. Battle would have to do as though he had had only the supplies and gear of his Comet Chaser One. "Rationing and stricter good management was to be administered," explained Rusty. Battle had crashed the Chaser that contained supplies that were more meager than what he had been given from the Hope Merchant freighter. "Your group will have to suffer because of the shortsightedness of the people in command," Rusty charged the counselor in a furtive sort of way. Battle signed off, recognizing the rebuke, with oaths and threatenings that was his ilk to do when denied.

Rusty shook his head and wondered how much of a burden was Battle's group going to cause humans and the local tribe's people. His actions could turn all of the indigenous people against all humans on the planet. "I hope the old cantankerous fool stays far away from any of the more cooperating colonists. Whoa is me."

CHAPTER THIRTY-ONE

The Riley Striker affair was settled amicably soon enough. The errant Riley was sentenced to a public whipping of three lashes. The sentence publicly was carried out the following day without any protestations from the earthlings. Only Eryka and Whisper made sounds of disapproval as the lashes were laid on Riley. Riley surprisingly wore the slightest of smiles as the sentence was carried out, as only he knew his actual intent of his actions. No doubt, he was relieved to get off so easy.

After this, the relationships of young people were of the very duteous and moralistic kind. Rusty and Evie both agreed in their private conversations that it would be natural for some of the young people to fall in love, marry and have children. This would be an accelerating factor to the settlement's growth and prosperity.

The days went by swiftly as Mawpics shared their ways with the earthlings. How to mine ore and make metal objects. Using coal with bellows was the primary way to extract metal and form it from the ore. They were also generous to teach about the domesticated animals in their possession, much to the joy of Whisper and Eryka. The two had become fast friends of late as Eryka with Whisper's help were teaching the Mawpics writing and reading.

Dirk and Midge with little Noel were the center of attention to everyone's delight. Noel was gaining weight and growing into a bouncing baby boy. After the capture of a planet goat with a kid to supply extra milk. The earthlings noticed that the Mawpics seemed to have a limited compliment of babies. Milk was now available to Noel. A milking bovine was also in the camp due to the generosity of the Mawpics.

When questioned at length the Mawpics related that many of their babies died before they attained a year old. When this circumstance was related to Dr. Wheeler she immediately set about to find the cause. If this cause could be determined, it would go a long way towards repairing the tacit rift between the two groups since the Riley affair.

Rexanne went about asking questions about the Mawpic's mother's habits and the baby's diet and circumstances. The young Mawpic mothers were cooperative, but the investigators could not find any cause of the wide spread mysterious infanticide. It was a tiring job because of the language impediments. Whisper and Eryka also helped, making copious notes and observations. Gloria assumed the animal husbandry of the new animals that the Mawpics had given the earthlings with some help from Whisper.

During this time, Bert was trying to be unobtrusive in his pursuit of Whisper as she scurried about helping Rexanne. Bert was convinced that Whisper should be his wife and spend his days with her for life. Whisper was like a butterfly flitting from one task to another making it difficult for Bert to court the young lady. Evie could see the signs and tried to help by talking to Eryka for any hints of a reciprocal nature on Whisper's part towards Bert. Eryka said, "Whisper is so intent with tasks and duties it appears courtship is not yet on her agenda. Please tell Bert to be patient and accommodating with the young Miss Winslet." Evie replied with her assent.

The time passed quickly as houses were built with much camaraderie and cooperation between the two groups. The integration was moving forward as a Mawpic father allowed his daughter to be courted by one changed Bristle Fume. Bristle had removed himself from the companionship of Riley Striker and had evolved into a decent individual with the coaching help of Rod and Sparks. These two men explained the facts of life on New Hope to Bristle and of our desire to follow the mores and tradition of a biblical nature. They also talked about the unusual circumstances here on the planet with other people's disciplines we would like to try and recognize After this man-to-man talk, Bristle was like another person especially after seeing Riley's incident.

The settlement was finished and looked like a village on earth in the nineteenth century. Rexanne had a surgery with her husband Rod as the town's busy Archeologist. The surgery was on Main Street. A foundry was built close to the stables with Dirk dare using a great hammer to the village's advantage. The equines given to them as gifts of peace and friendship by the Mawpics were kept in the stables. Rusty and Evie established a general store. They supplied it from the stores brought from Hope Merchant and used as a barter system to start the economy moving. When a certain amount of order had been established, Rusty called a meeting of his group and the five Mawpic leaders.

The reason for the gathering was explained so that the Mawpics could enter in with suggestions or could refuse any participation. Joel and Evie had formulated an initial document that only needed fine-tuning to be acceptable to all present. (A constitution and a code of ethics.) The Mawpics liked the ideas but reserved the right to have their people review the document and approve or reject it in its present form. Rusty and company approved the constitution with its list of rights for the individual. An interim government or council would rule until the settlement grew large enough to support an elected bicameral body for laws and a high court to render interpretations. By popular vote and nominations Rusty was to be the first and only Supreme Court judge. Joel, Bert, Whisper, and Garner were chosen to be the governing council.

The dying of many of the Mawpic's children was determined to be a small nut. A local tasty chewy nut that the woman chewed for pain relief and to allay sickness was full of selenium and belladonna causing miscarriages. When Rexanne told the Mawpic's of the cause and that they should not chew the nut, the women were distressed and reluctant to cease the tradition.

Much to the chagrin of their new settlement the Mawpics never returned to implement the new constitution or to continue to acclimate the earthlings to their new environment. When Rusty and Joel made a trip to the Mawpic village, at the far end of the plateau, out of normal sight, the two were surprised to see that it was gone. It was thought that too many changes and suggestions by the humans caused the Mawpic's dispersion. Lock, stock, and barrel were missing including one of their own, Bristle Fume. They area was bare, swept clean of all occupancy and presence. Not even a trace was left to indicate in what direction they might have traveled. Their exit was both complete and mysterious. Rusty and Joel returned to the New Hope settlement with the distressing news.

It was so strange because the animals left behind by the mawpics, were blending with the Earth animals bringing, a new gene pool to the existing stock. Why would the Mawpics leave behind the animals, loaned tools, and other things of value? This planet, named Patelles, was exhibiting unusual happenings. Rumblings and shaking became daily occurrences. "Nothing to be concerned about as the instruments indicted all activity was in the southern hemisphere far, far away," said Bert

The root people and the water people, both were apparently antagonistic towards the earthlings at first sight and the Mawpics so compatible with human behavior and physical attributes, all mysteriously. The new governing council met and decided that it would be in the best interest of the new settlement, New Hope, to stay and complete their original assignment. After all, the animals were multiplying, Noel was growing, and Bert and Whisper were apparently courting. A real good start after a rather unsettled, bizarre beginning.

The village was built on a slight rise from the rest of the plateau. Each plot had some trees for shade from the planet's sun. The sun was almost of a pink shade, and the evening sunsets were spectacular. Each house was made of a combination of materials both brought and local. The freighter was still close by and was established as a sanctuary when violent storms came upon the landscape at infrequent intervals. It also contained sophisticated communication equipment for possible deep space contacts.

Battle called at regular intervals trying to get Rusty or Bert to come half way to provide some more supplies. Battle was told to manage his own resources to keep themselves fed and protected from the elements. "Shoot some deer, catch some fish, and learn to walk a lot," said Rusty with some authority. The contacts eventually, ended.

Soon after a judicious time when the settlement was on a good footing, it was decreed that a search party would be assembled and sent out to try and relocate the missing Mawpics, including Bristle Fume. The group was made up of Rusty, Joel, Gloria, and Dirk, leaving Bert in charge. They were requested to keep in contact and take no unnecessary chances. The trek might be very dangerous. On a cool autumn morning, the little band set off with as many supplies they could carry for an extended search. After only one day on the search Gloria had to return for she was apparently pregnant. Consequently, Garner Trapp was selected to make up the foursome, tasked with unraveling the mystery of the missing Mawpics. Again, the four departed from camp with a send off of anxious proportions.

CHAPTER THIRTY-TWO

The going was very easy for the four as they trudged over the near level plateau terrain. At first, they traveled slowly in great circles about what they thought was the Mawpic's old village site, looking for any sign of many feet traveling away from the village site. The great circle subsequently came to a place on the plateau where the way was either up into the mountains or down in the valleys. The four trying to decide which way to go, held a confab. Each member gave their thoughts as to the likelihood which way the Mawpics would go. Garner's idea seemed to be the one that convinced them to go down in the valley.

"The Mawpics would not want go into the mountains because of the coming cold and the trek would slow them down as well as I see snow up there."

Garner finish by saying, "Which ever way we go it will be a test of our endurance and investigating skills."

Joel made com-link contact back to the village to tell them of their decision to descend into the valley to extend the search area down there. Joel signed off with a familiar comment.

"We are going down into the unknown but will return with the known."

With these words, trailing off in the breezes the four began the arduous task of searching and descending the valley trail. About half way down, Joel found some proof of previous travelers. The evidence was a wad of sweet Chicle-like gum, from the offending nut earlier, that was chewed by the Mawpics men for energy and the women for pain relief etc. Young Bristle Fume had also gotten into the habit chewing the sweet nut plant for a physical lift. The wad was still slightly moist at its discovery.

"Somebody has recently taken this trail down into the valley," said Joel while rubbing his chin in deep thought. "It might have been our own Bristle giving us some clue as to the departing Mawpics."

After touching the wad gingerly Garner came to the same conclusion. "This stuff is unhealthy but earthlings are also noted for consuming stuff that greatly hinders their health. It is rather obvious that this was to be found. Maybe it is bait for a trap to lead us on to some sort of confrontation where we would be out numbered and defeated." Garner gave this opinion with up raised arms as a sign of frustration. Joel was also hesitant to move forward as they had earlier, with regular voices and no stealth in their progress.

Dirk finally spoke up as a new father might. "I will tell you fellows that we had better be more careful on this trek than before because it certainly appears that these Mawpics can be a crafty bunch of customers."

Rusty replied with a smile on his lips. "Maybe it is Bristle that has become the spitting image of his new friends, like earthlings."

Joel brought them back to the chore at hand.

"We must continue with great care and see if we can locate the fleeing Mawpics so we can intelligently relate all to the council for any further action. Let's continue and be more vigilant than before."

With finality to the conversation, Rusty began again to lead carefully the group down the valley trail. No further sign was discovered as they reached the valley floor where they stopped to rest and call back to Bert with their report.

Rusty told of their find of a sweet wad on the trail. He also related that in the valley, it was lush with trees and other vegetation. "A locality that would be very difficult to reconnoiter." Bert's only comment was to be extremely careful in any further discovery. "We will continue to follow the Mawpics for one more day. If no success we will return to the village,"said Rusty.

Garner Trapp said when Rusty had finished the transmission, "I think I smell smoke or is it just my imagination?"

No one answered immediately as each turned their noses up in the air vigorously sniffed the air for possible confirmation. No one sensed the same odor as Garner, but each one said that if he could give a direction they could begin to travel in that direction. With that kind of confirmation the group of four started to move through the trees and under-growth, looking for any signs of recent travel. It was hard going for the group and their meticulous searching slowed them down considerably. Dirk made the first find.

"Over here. I have found some footprints that indicate a recent passing."

The others came to Dirk's side. They agreed that to locate any traces of the Mawpic's trail they should travel in single file to decrease any chances of discovery, triple checking the trail, off to one side. They had been bunched up in twos and threes for camaraderie or inherent safety.

"Now the last person in the Mawpic's line must clean the trail of prints by brushing and thrashing the trails telltale foot prints with tree branches. Their thrasher must have been distracted at this point by something or someone," informed Dirk. "I see prints that are not ours."

"The prints seem to be rather recent," opined Joel as he rubbed the bridge of his nose as though his opinion would be apparent to his colleagues. The prints are quite large so maybe Bristle had been in charge of the thrashing the trail," said Joel with a twinkle in his eyes for he knew that Bristle was not too smart and small in stature but with big, wide feet.

Garner was quick to correct the jest. "It had to be a Mawpic for they all have large feet because of going barefoot all their lives."

Joel had to have the last opinion. "Bristle had a shuffling gait as these tracks show. He was probably too tired to accomplish his thrashing job."

Rusty said with some exasperation in his voice, "all right you guys, let's stop the chic-chat, and get on with this operation."

With that friendly chastisement, the four once again moved forward with stealth and astute diligence.

After several hours, they came upon the Mawpic bivouac almost by chance. Dirk had left the group to attend to some necessary function and stumbled upon the Mawpic's outer camp perimeter. He was still undetected and slowly crept back to the other three searchers. When he had been reunited with them, he put his index finger up to his lips to indicate silence. In a husky whisper, he related that he had found the Mawpic Camp. "It is about fifty meters away."

Dirk described what he had seen to the dismay of the small group. They knew they were out-numbered maybe as much as twenty to one, but Rusty kept a victory face and showed no dismay at the news.

Garner first whispered, "all right, what do we do now?"

The question seemed to be fundamental because the operation was to find them and ascertain why they had left, thought Garner. Of course being here with four persons facing a disturbed, and fleeing group of indigenous people had an effect that Joel was not accustomed to. It wasn't fear or cowardice; it was the respect for the unknown and untested. Sweat ran down the face of Joel as he contemplated on what they would do next. It was the sweat of patience.

"The first thing to do," said Rusty, "is to notify Bert to see if he thinks we should come back or attempt some sort of contact with the Mawpics. After all, he holds the colony in the palm of his hand, so to speak. The tribal group showed no real menacing signs when on the plateau."

All heads nodded in approval as the group eased farther back into some cover provided by thick vegetation. Rusty had the com-link and began to send his message. The volume was turned way down but all could hear the answer that Bert was suggesting.

"If you have ample supplies for a longer stay, try to reconnoiter in the area to determine if they seem offensive or agitated to hinder our future contact. Spying out for Bristle would give some indication of their mood. If he is free, and unharmed it might indicate that the Mawpics are not so disturbed as we might think. The people here at base camp are worried about all of you. Can I tell them of your abbreviated progress?"

"Yes. Good advice." Rusty agreed. The little group of four set about making plans.

CHAPTER THIRTY-THREE

The days at New Hope village were peaceful, and tranquil at the settlement. It was enjoyed for some period of time. The only thing the settlers experienced was a sense of loneliness and anxiety over four missing comrades. Some talk about trying to return to their own galaxy but when the facts were known the talk subsided. They might not have enough fuel to return to earth but if they could get back to Galaxy One where a communication buoy was located they could send out a distress signal. Then someone would find them there and return them to earth on the finder's fee and with more fuel. This idea was shot down when the odds of being found in an old galaxy buoy were so high, which would condemn them to certain death because of the unsanctioned trip and the so called abduction of Battle's daughter. The lack of substantial fuel was the clincher for all talk of returning anywhere. That thought died a peaceful demise.

Bert spent much of his time being upbeat about their present circumstances. Bert and Evie would go about the village with positive talk and suggestions on how to keep busy with new events. This led the women to form a committee on beautification of the surrounding area by planting scrubs and bushes that would bear fruit and flowers on this new planet. Soon, New Hope was anticipating the beauty and berries that the bushes would eventually provide.

It was amazing how the plant life flourished in such short periods of time. The soil was so rich that anything they planted grew with a boundless alacrity. The reason for the local plantings seemed obvious. The distant areas were rich in fruit and berries to such an extent, the settlers had their fill for a definite time, but as the colony grew the distant areas would become depleted. The animal life at New Hope was also very plenteous. Prairie Chicken Delight was on the menu of most of the people, but when a community get-together was arranged, a local hog of the tasty variety was roasted over an open pit. Many being found in the dense growth of vegetation.

The group of four where sorely missed as they had not been heard of for an extended period time. It was assumed the group had run into foul luck, and no one wanted to venture out to try and located them. Bert reasoned if more people were sent out, more could be lost.

The ship was stationery now as a supply depot and had limited sub light fuel to make any effective reconnaissance. It was a sad situation for Gloria especially since her pregnancy was a false positive. She moped about wanting someone or anyone to try and find Joel's group. Evie and Bert Bright tried to reason with the others of the dangers associated with another exploratory trek to find the lost tribe of Mawpics and to ascertain what had happened to the absent group of four. This view was met with some opposite ideas.

"Another group of four could at least follow any sign or the trail left by our people and with great stealth determine what has happened to our loved ones," postulated Gloria with emotion rising up in her voice. "I for one would like to at least try. It is better than just sitting around here and never knowing what happened."

Evie and Bert could not fault this opinion. Soon after this exchange, it was decided that four more villagers would try and locate the missing members of the first group. The village met, and the following members volunteered to form up an a search party for rescue or determination. Fairly, Gloria, Whisper, and Victor who had stayed behind from Battle's group, were all sanctioned to make the trip for better or worse. This time the party took a variety of weapons and much offensive paraphernalia, providing them with an impressive strike force if needed. Staying behind, Bert was still in the leadership position and Evie was his backup or second in command.

Bert had the group go through some basic maneuvers and instructions the day before they left. Gloria was early on the scene as a person with a very high stake in the outcome of this expedition. Her suggestions and encouragement flowed like a drill sergeant. Everyone took it in good humor knowing how much she missed and loved her Joel. After hours of training the group in the fundamentals of combat, the four were sent off early the following morning with prayers for safety and success. Midge gave each member a token to remind them of their task and of her reliance on their success for her future. The token was a miniature wooden doll with the likeness of Dirk formed as best as Midge could fashion. "This will remind you of the reason you are going on the excursion," Midge expressed with heartfelt emotion as the four moved out across the plateau as her Dirk and three others had done many days before.

The little band could follow the trail very easily across the plateau geography, though many hollows and dales were on their route. The days was picture perfect for the stroll across the plateau, enjoyed by the party of four especially Victor and Whisper. Victor acting likes a big and older brother towards Whisper. An avuncular relationship that was casual and benign. Their dedication to the tasks equaled the others even though they had not the same investment as Gloria and Fairly.

Whisper's attraction to Bert was evident to all but Rusty. Evie had mentioned it to Rusty but he shrugged it off as insignificant. "Women are always looking for romance when none exists," was Rusty's first comment but eventually after observing the two interacting in projects and work details at base, soon changed his mind. Rusty, earlier said he would have a long talk with Bert about marriage and the covenants that accompanied that estate when they returned. It was too late now as Rusty had left before and was now in a lower valley of Patelles.

It took about a day to transverse the plateau and purchases the trail that led down into the great valley below. This was a good place to make camp, thought Victor as the four had hurried most of the day with their heavy equipment on their backs making the trek fatiguing.

"Let's set up our camp on this ledge overlooking the great valley below, "said Victor with his command voice in place but not too severe. This will give us a time to use our elecnoculars for locating any movement or warm blooded beings in the forest below."

With this tempting possibility in mind, the crew busily made camp as well as supper before the sunset and darkness prevailed with a dark blanket of cool night air. When all appetites had been satisfied, each member took out of their equipment packs, elecnoculars that could scan the darkness of the valley below for any life forms.

This exercise also had them turn to the sky and its many celestial forms for study and conversation. The planet's two moons had not yet appeared on the horizon to add extra light to the dazzling, starry display. The sky looked nothing like earth's heavens with its air pollution. Many stars shining like sparks and giving the impression one could reach up and catch one like a lightening fly. The stars were brighter not only because of little or no pollution but also because they all appeared to be much closer in distance. A reality or only an optical illusion. As the four sat about the camp, with the fire now only embers, Whisper laid her head on Gloria's lap and asked, "do you think we will ever see normal times again?"

"Of course we will, funny little girl," answered Gloria with real affection in her motherly voice. .

"Lets each give any reports or suggestions about what we will see and what to do next." Gloria struggled to get up as she addressed the little group, trying to get everyone back to the issue at hand, just as the two moons began to peek over the horizon.

With no positive sightings or reports yet, it was up to Victor to finalize the day's activities. Let's get to sleep, as tomorrow will be a big day going down the trail into the valley.

Victor volunteered to take the first watch of night guard duty.

CHAPTER THIRTY-FOUR

"Everything happens to me," uttered Battle Winslet as he surveyed his land car that had given up the ghost at last. The old commander had loaded up his land car and with his special compliment of people and a load of provisions. He set out to cross the planet's continent in the Northern Hemisphere. It was a daunting task he knew, but everything had gone wrong where he and his band had tried to settle on Patelles. No one wanted to work or exert themselves; most notable was Battle and his son, Waver. Blenda was trying to keep the settlement together but without much luck or help. Finally, in desperation the group acquiesced to Battle's directive to break camp and head west towards the other humans. The food was low, and the camp supplies were running out. They needed to have someone to work the animals and harvest food, but no volunteers The king and his son as well as close friends avoided work as it was beneath their station to toil for these essentials. When the inevitable failure was in sight, Battle surmised if he could just get to the other humans, they could provide all that was needed for a comfortable existence on this lonely and wild planet.

On a beautiful morning, Battle had the group stowed all the gear that they could on the land car They all headed west towards Rusty and Bert's settlement. It was an ugly sight. The one land car was over loaded to afford luxury to the few who rode the vehicle while the rest walked beside the monstrosity with backpacks loaded to hilt. The terrain was very unforgiving for the first week of travel. Streams were forded and hills gained only by varying degrees of pushing the land car by the lowly plebeians. After about a week of this kind of traveling Battle made a rest stop to chastise the burden carriers for their slowness It was bad enough to foment a mutiny.

CHAPTER THIRTY FIVE

At about 12 o'clock, Victor awakened Whisper to take the next watch as she had previously volunteered. After leaving her warm sleep pad she continued to awaken by splashing her face with some water, and then leaving a few yawns behind, Whisper took up her watch on a higher vantage point than the camp. The air was cool, and the stars and the moons gave off an eerie glow that was not like earth's moon. Whisper settled down with her stun gun on her lap. It was a time of reflection as well as a heightened attention to all the sights and sounds the night afforded.

Whisper had not realized she missed her mother until just now. She could talk to Gloria or Evie, but it was not the same. New feelings had begun to rise up in the young woman's body and mind. It was hard not to share this with her mother who was so understanding and wise. Whisper had been close to her mom but the fact that Battle and Waver demanded so much of Blenda's time made the mother

-daughter bond tenuous. Whisper resigned herself to play the waiting game and see what happens in the days ahead.

Looking at her watch to see that the two hours had passed more quickly than she had realized, Whisper took one last look around the area of the camp. Determining that all was well she sought out Fairly to take the next watch. She found Fairly at her sleeping pod but hesitated because of her deep sleep with light snoring. She thought that to wake her would be cruel because of the heavy burdens Fairly had been carrying. Her head told her to wake Victor and have a talk with him which would be a better option. Her reasoning was slightly biased by her brotherly feelings for Victor. She had been open around him when they were working together on projects and work details. She gave no hint of her need for brotherly fellowship to the older man, but she was now determined on this mission to be a real sister and helper to Victor.

Finding the older leader of this mission, she tugged at his shoulder to arouse him to wakefulness. "Victor, wake up for a turn at sentry duty. I was unable to bring myself to wake up Fairly as she was sleeping so soundly." Victor turned over and looked into the face of Whisper and her concern for Fairly. He smiled and said, "I haven't been sleeping very deep so your timing is about perfect. I need to get up and make plans for today's journey. How are you doing? You appear to be concerned about something. A furrowed brow above your eyes gives me cause to ask, what is the matter?"

A surprised and gracious Whisper replied with honesty. "I have been thinking about a lot of things that I could not think about when we were so busy back at the settlement. Things like the future and relationships"

Victor got up and looked down at Whisper as he answered. "It will all turn out all right in the end. Take these things one day at a time."

Victor left and climbed the little knoll for his turn at sentry duty. Whisper sought out her sleep pad and tried to sleep in the few hours before dawn. 'Growing up is so difficult in these times,' Whisper thought as slumber finally washed over her, taking her to a place of tranquility and satisfaction of fulfilling proportions. A place of love and warm feelings, without the possibility of dire or unforeseen consequences.

When the dawn arrived with skies so blue and clouds so white, the four gathered for a breakfast meal and talked of the coming day. Victor and Fairly were apparently well rested and ready for the long hike down the plateau. Whisper and Gloria were quiet and still tried to cast off any sleepiness that tried to linger. When the meal was completed and all gear packed up tight and neat, Victor gave brief instructions to the group.

"We go down with as much stealth as possible, Each person must be on the lookout for anything that might give us a clue to what has happened on this trail, now and earlier. Any unusual mark or sign is to be examined meticulously. Above all, make no sound and try to leave little evidence of our advance. I don't think we will see anything or anybody this day, but we can't be too confident about our movements."

The trail was well used. It had been an animal trail at first thought Victor. Now it was well worn with travel by Mawpics or others like them. Stones dislodged, branches broken, leaves missing on limbs. No doubt, humans made some. The group moved quietly but steadily down into the great valley below. It took all day to reach a relative level area near the valley floor. A good place to stop as the day was well spent.

Fairly and Victor selected a spot away from the trail to make camp for the night. It was grassy and level with an overhang of rock above their heads for some protection from rain. The spot was also backing into a small cleft that provided cover from any winds. It was far enough away from the trail so that anyone traveling on it would not discover the camp. As preparations for their late meal were being made, Whisper discovered some sign that indicated they were not the first ones to use this site for a camp. A small fire pit had been covered to disguise its existence and well as traces of several lean-tos's of grass and branches. Closer inspection revealed a footprint, but all other traces had been well covered. It was decided that it was a camp of Mawpics. "Probably a small group that could have been a rear guard for their exit from the plateau. A group that was in such a hurry to join their friends they did not disguise the remains of their camp," said Victor with outstretched arms towards the evidence.

Victor took the first Sentry and Whisper the second. Gloria was happy to take the last duty after Fairly, about two hours each. It was a quiet camp. It was very peaceful with the dark but star filled sky. It still revealed little because of the low growing trees and brush. The four lay on their backs on the grassy park and ventured into some deep conversation while looking up at the unfamiliar starry sky. A time when the innermost thoughts of humans seemed to float to the top of the brain and spill out the mouth. Hopes and fears radiated in the dark surroundings of a planet still of unknown qualities. A time of reflection. Each member learned more about each other in those hours before the sleeping hour than all the days spent in the New Hope village. It was a time of cleansing as well as being informative for each to be encouraged in the days to come. The conversations were deep and cathartic.

The night passed uneventful as daylight brought a new sense of camaraderie. Breakfast was cheery as the group looked at each other with new eyes. Packing up and pushing on with same cautions as before, the little band moved further down the trail into the great valley of uncertainties. Today would bring them to the valley floor and a new sense of stealth as they searched for clues about the missing group of four and the Mawpics from their earlier ranks.

The air became heavy as the humidity rose. The cause must be a coming rain or a watercourse was near. The trail revealed no new clues but all felt they were on the right track.

Victor was in the lead when he first saw it. He signaled for all to stop and urging them to examine the sign. Blood was always something that got the attention of investigators.

CHAPTER THIRTY-SIX

Victor held up the leafy foliage that had blood smeared on it. The first thought was that it was human but further searches showed that a small animal like a rabbit, complete with a discarded snare, had been caught and butchered for someone's repast. With this conclusion, the four went on down the trail with new concerns about whom and what they were trailing. The death of anything was a sobering event.

When the planet's sun had reached its zenith, the group became uncomfortable because of the heat and humidity. Insects buzzed about their heads coupled with sweat that began to hinder their advance. Victor called a halt and purchased some shade in a clump of trees not far from the trail. A time of refreshment with food and drink to match the day's conditions. Victor was the oldest so he suggested Whisper climb one of the trees for a better observation of the surrounding territory. All agreed to his proposal.

Victor picked out a tree with appropriate branches and indicated her appointed ascent. The tree was very accommodating with branches in a symmetrical and climbable pattern. Whisper was able to reach very high in the tree before she began her running commentary of the surrounding geographical features.

"I can see a lot of territory from up here. The plateau is very high and looks to be quite a distance that we have traveled. I can see what appears to be the absolute bottom of the valley. A river runs into a finger lake at the bottom. The lake is very long and surrounded with vegetation of all kinds. A mist is rising in the distance where the river takes up again from the lake. It is probably a waterfall. Wait! I think I can see a small rise of smoke from the lake's furthermost shore and it is not a waterfall, I am sure. I forgot to bring the elecnoculars. I will come down for a better look with the elecnoculars.

As Whisper scrambled down the tree, Gloria was up in it climbing to meet her. She had two sets of elecnoculars and would get a look for herself at the top. She gave little attention to the cautions of Victor from below scolding, "what are you doing?" Gloria would not be denied the chance of locating the Mawpic's camp first, with the four missing searchers. With the dexterity of a monkey the young woman passed Whisper on her way up the tree to it's highest attainable branches. Others thought it to be precarious, but Gloria had no thought of herself in the discovery of their quarry. She began a commentary on her observations.

"I can see what appears to be smoke rising from the shoreline of the lake. Whisper was correct in her earlier assessment. It is only a wisp but it is steady. The faintest of paths or trails lead in that direction and it has seen some recent use. My elecnoculars have now caught the image of native beings around the base of the fire area. I am certain this is the resting camp of the Mawpics, even though there is much activity. Who else could it be?"

From below, the listening group began to form a plan of action as Whisper and Gloria descended the great tree. Victor was adamant that the group did not split up as was suggested by Gloria in a hasty manner. Victor felt that the others wanted to lead a spearhead to determine the Mawpics strength and or intentions towards outsiders. "We will keep together for strength and safety," was Victor's final comment. Gloria was not disheartened by her plan being rejected. The group was once again in one accord as the plan was revealed by Victor as the best course of action.

"We will move down as close as is safe while there still is light. Afterwards when dark, will make a stealthy advance close enough to make further assessments on the situation."

Off they went with care and stealth. The trail they followed soon led them to the lakeshore. The area was filled with coniferous and hardwood trees. The air became very warm and humid to the surprise of the four. The sky was beginning to bleed away towards the far horizon, above the Mawpics location. Reds and pinks bled into the sunset as though the horizon was on fire. The beauty of the sunset belied the precarious position of four very alert searchers.

It was very quiet for some strange reason. The four moved along the shore with care because of the exposure on the lakeside. Trying to keep from exposing any silhouette, they kept to a low profile. When their advance had purchased a place only about 100 meters from their target, they followed Victor into a depression that slanted uphill. This gave the group a place to hide until the nighttime rolled over the valley. They hunkered down and in silence waited for Victor's signal to continue.

The air changed to cool as the night slowly made darkness a friend. A heavy dew was settling down to make the way quiet but moist. Victor had a huddle explaining his strategy to advance to the campsite and gather what information they could at this time. Voices heard would tend to tell us if anger or threatening were on their agenda. Each member murmured agreement and comprehension. It was quiet because all of the tribe was resting as though the day had been fatiguing. Eventually, darkness fell like a curtain when Victor signed to move forward by spreading out.

This was a time that Whisper wished she had her dog, Pep, with her for help in the nose and ear department. As Whisper moved forward with stealth and care, she noticed that the area she was in had an unusual fragrance. When she experienced a number of scratches and tears in her clothing, she quickly realized she was in a patch of wild rose bushes. This would slow her down considerably, causing her to lag behind the other's advancement. It would be repugnant not to complete her task as part of the team. With cupped ear, she realized that the others were far to the left of her making actions to be careless in her advance. After what seemed to be an eternity she stopped to access her wounds and torn clothing. She felt woozy and sweaty so she lay in a cool grassy area she had finally acquired. Laying there in the night's coolness, she realized how torn and ragged she must be. She felt the warm ooze of blood on her face and arms and tried to wipe the areas clean with no success. As she was trying to clean up her self, she heard the hue and cry of her comrades as they were apparently being captured on the outskirts of the camp. Straining to see through the sweat and blood of her forehead, she was able to see the Mawpic's sentries take her friends to the center of the camp.

Whisper was upset, and half crazed when she saw Gloria and Fairly being manhandled by several large Mawpics. She was certain she could do little to help her friends in her condition now. No sense trying to go back to the plateau. Her thoughts were such that she wanted to move forward and be with Gloria and the others, thereby giving an edge in the thought processes for escape, later.

Whisper with real resolve, rose up and began to walk towards the center of the campsite. Losing a shoe in the tangles of vines, she limped into the camp like a scene out of some scary play. It was then all the Mawpics were struck dumb. The scene was one of complete silence and fear as the young woman advanced with blood smeared all over her body. Her torn clothes and bloody appearance complete with her limping made several Mawpics fall down and bow in servitude. The others soon followed suit. The entire assembled tribe bowed and scraped with the apparent arrival of a deity. With gasps of relief, her friends greeted her in like manner to fortify what ever was going on. The indigenous people seemed to view Whisper as some sort of female goddess. They bowed and scraped with an awesome reverence. Their women brought out regal finery that Whisper put on with a flair leaving her ruined apparel to be burned. The three confined humans became important and treated with a new esteem with privileges. All confines removed with a degree of kindness not expected by the three humans. All were glad that Whisper arrived and was alive and animated. Very Glad!

CHAPTER THIRTY-SEVEN

The land car had a limited supply of fuel left from the folly of the previous directors. The car was laden with the fuel containers and only one small operator. Blenda handled the wheel with gusto as they began the journey across the rest of the continent. The fellows carried backpacks, and the women were burdened with pack baskets slung over their shoulders, one on each side. The march westward was reminiscence of pioneer days back on earth long, long ago. The plains did not present too many obstacles, but the rivers were quite a challenge. Rafts had to be built to carry the car and supplies over the watery barriers. The deserts were another matter. At these points, food as well as water became very short in supply, causing short tempers and angry exchanges. This Trek made even the earlier miscreants work and toil a little.

Carl and Walter tried to keep order as Waver and Battle again led the charge of accusatory remarks or gestures. Blenda was constantly intervening with her soothing words of wisdom and intelligence. It was on one of these occasions that the troupe was set upon by angry hostiles. As tempers rose with loud outbursts by battle and Waver, an arrow sailed into the participants and caught Porc square in the back end, causing a painful wound. The others hit the ground and kept close to the car for protection.

When Carl and Walter established the source of the grievous missiles, they both fired their stun guns to the consternation of the hostiles. One-targeted hostile rose up in agony, then slumping over appearing dead, caused his comrades to begin to melt away. It was not to be a final act on the part of the hostiles as they continued to harass the group from time to time from safe vantage points until darkness fell on the exhausted humans.

In the dark, the group kept a close watch on any moves that might be made by the hostiles. Only Battle Winslet was resting comfortably and thinking of ways to regain control over the group. It would require drastic means to eliminate Carl and Walter as co-leaders, by tacit approval. Battle was certain that only brute force and terror tactics would accomplish the take over by him. "We should all rush them and wipe them off the face of this planet," was Battle's war cry. Waver and Porc could help when he recovered from his wounds and would be available. With great shouts of deafening savagery by three or more humans, the Hostiles apparently let up on their harassment.

Battle Winslet was only slightly irritated as Carl and Walter joined forces to repair the land car, again. Battle wanted to ride the car even if in poor shape. Carl gave his opinion about the patched land car. "One more time of repairs on this old buggy, and we will have to use string and wire instead of spare parts. It would be a great help if all of the party would walk instead of riding." Battle was getting accustomed to others giving orders as he rested in the shade of an old tree. It was only a short time before Battle realized he had lost his edge as commander and accepted the unspoken title of Counselor Emeritus. The following days and nights were filled with mystery and intrigue as Battle and his cadre willingly worked with the traveling group.

Carl and Walter finished repairing the land car one more time as best they could, as others found food and packed it for travel. Only Battle, Waver, and Porc hung back in the shadow of the big tree. Their hands were clean, but their stomachs growled as the foodstuffs were not shared with the slackers. After only a day or two, the slackers became workers, and helpers to complement the preparations for the long haul ahead.

The land car had a limited supply of fuel left from the folly of the previous directors. The car was laden with the fuel containers and only one small operator. Blenda handled the wheel with gusto as they began the journey across the rest of the continent. Battle and Waver stuck to the running boards ignoring Carl's suggestion. The fellows carried backpacks, and the women were burdened with pack baskets slung over their shoulders, one on each side. The march westward was reminiscence of pioneer days back on earth long, long ago. The plains did not present too many obstacles, but the rivers were quite a challenge. Rafts had to be built to carry the car and supplies over the watery barriers. The deserts were another matter. At these points, food as well as water became short in supply causing short tempers and angry exchanges. . In the dark, the group kept a close watch on any moves that might be made by the hostiles. Only Battle Winslet was resting comfortably and thinking of ways to regain control over the group. It would require drastic means to eliminate Carl and Walter as co leaders. Battle was certain that only brute force and terror tactics would accomplish the take over. Waver and Porc could help when he recovered from his wounds.

Porc and Waver became close friends to the apprehension of Blenda and others. The two boys were what one would call slackers. This also encouraged mischief of the most irritating kind. There came a day when several rafts had to be built to cross a small but swift river. To get out of some heavy work of felling trees, the boys volunteered to lash the timbers together for the raft floor. With naughty singing and jostling each other, they pretentiously attempted at laboriously tying the timbers with some rope they made from vines and river grasses. When finished, Carl and Walter suggested that the boys and Battle go first in the Boy's raft with some of their own possessions. With some hesitantly protestations from the boys, they gingerly boarded the craft. They really wanted to be first across which was a given for the three slackers. Hopping on board with restrained fanfare, they pushed off into the swift water. Three boys originally wanted Carl or Walter to utilize the craft. Deep down they were aware of its tenuous construction. With stifled shouts of victory and with up raised arms, the three were promptly thrown into the water, as the raft broke apart as predicted by Carl on shore. Rescuing the three was a complicated and tiring exercise by Walter and Carl and a few others. They brought the three on shore with muted thanks from three soaked louts but also with oaths aimed at each other for implied stupidity and shoddy construction.

The following days and nights were filled with mystery and intrigue, as Battle and his cadre appeared to be tranquil and in conformity with everyone. Was peace going to be a permanent phenomenon?

CHAPTER THIRTY-EIGHT

The days were very lazy as well as very productive at the lake camp. The Mawpics kept very busy with their annual catching and processing the fish from the lake. Both salting and smoking were employed to keep the meat from spoiling. It was without explanation that the fishing and smoking event did not include the new colonists. During this time, another apparently friendly tribe of indigenous people came to the area with the four missing colonists. The Kampacs were a friendly tribe of peoples that had cared for and instructed the four humans for the last several days of travel and sharing. The four had been intercepted by the Kampacs and were included in the tribe's activities. Hunting, fishing, mining had kept the four in tow and occupied so that escape or communication was not a high priority.

The eight reunited colonists entered into a joyous get-together. Joel, Rusty, Garner, and Dirk were all in good spirits from their recent trip into the lower interior of this area, with the Kampacs. Whisper explained to her friends her newly found importance among the Mawpics and her very rich attire she was wearing, to the four reunited settlers. She was the talk of the encampment as some Mawpics tried to make her out as a goddess or at least a princess of the deep and dark world of Shandowee, the power force of the volcanoes of the southern hemisphere that rumbled and shook on occasion. At the very least, her visit had made the inhabitants of this area to be very cautious and courteous to the eight humans in their midst.

The only disquieting event was the little dolls that Midge made had been seize by the natives and used as offerings or sacrifices to the lake when a net was used to gather fish. The human held their tongues to wait and see if other unusual action where in the native's Agenda.

After a great feast and a festival-like evening, all the participants finally retired for the night. It became known that the Mawpic's hasty retreat from the plateau was because the fishing rite was at hand and very important. It only came once a year. Leaving no clues about their plateau camp was what they did as a habit to foil any antagonists from locating the tribe. It also was a time to mingle with the friendly Kampacs for trading or marriage possibilities

It was at this time the men began to lay a plan for returning to their settlement on the plateau. Rusty was adamant that they return as soon as possible. The com-links had also been appropriated by the natives and were either hidden or destroyed. He didn't ask about them for possible tribal annoyance.

Rusty had a feeling in his bones that trouble may soon visit the New Hope settlement. It appeared to Joel that winter months of unknown weather might arrive without being sufficiently prepared. With these thoughts in mind, the eight earthlings began by saying goodbyes and accepting gifts in the morning. (No carved dolls of Midges labor were among the gifts or com-links.)

Before leaving, Bristle Fume the wayward human, asked to talk to Rusty Bolt in private for a moment. Going off a little ways Rusty and Bristle spoke in hushed tones for only a moment and then returned to the assembled group of colonists. With what might be viewed as feigned sadness from the indigenous peoples, the eight settlers started on their return trek to the plateau and their comrades. Bristle was not in sight.

The day was brilliant with sunshine and white puffy clouds floating across the sky in a succession of shapes and forms. Rusty had taken the lead as Victor brought up the rear. The group of eight looked back several times to determine if any possible hostile activities that the Mawpics and Kampacs, might initiate. The targeted groups below appeared to be in natural modes of occupation and activity.

In Rusty's mind was the thought of the tribe's opinion that Whisper was some kind of deity that they really didn't want her to leave. If the tribes wanted they could easily overtake the eight colonists and return Whisper to their bosom as a goddess of good fortune and prosperity. (Maybe the dolls would do the same.) Rusty quickly put into action a quick pace as soon as they had found a place of concealment from the two tribes of local peoples. He was certain that Bristle Fume would be all right, as he had been officially initiated into the Mawpics when he married his Mawpic lady. Nevertheless, Rusty was suspicious of the locals because when they left, the Mawpics and Kampacs only gave the colonists a one-day's supply of provisions. The send off was with great fanfare and strained generosity .The tribes' mask of exuberance concerning Whisper's leaving was not hidden well. Keeping these concerns to himself, Rusty lead his band with an urgency noted by Whisper who had taken her place just behind Rusty.

"Rusty why are we in such a hurry to leave this beautiful region?"

It was a question Rusty did not want to explain right then but Whisper was insistent. Finally, Rusty replied that he had an eerie feeling about the colonist up on the plateau and wanted to return as quickly as possible. "I feel that danger in some form is trying to negate all we have accomplished, be it winter weather or local peoples I don't feel good about this long of a separation of our people." This was truthful and satisfied the young woman's inquisitiveness for now.

The day was rather cool but very clear. The path led up the to the plateau. Like so many visuals, it was much steeper and more arduous when viewed from down below. Frequent stops were the order of the day as well as omitting a noontime lunch break. At the end of the day, Rusty had the group stop for food and rest. A very secluded spot was found with the rocks behind them and a thick clump of trees before them. Rusty tried to articulate his reasoning for the safety and caution he thought was needed. The group listened intensely.

"My reasoning is that the Mawpics and Kampacs only gave us one day's supply of food. Their send off was rather stilted, as was some dialogue I over-heard concerning the fact that more mouths might deplete their food supply. Wanting Whisper for a worshiped deity to allay the displeasure of the Shandowee spirit of volcanoes. I would rather act on the side of caution in these circumstances causing us little discomfort for the safety it will afford."

Only Whisper commented. "Your observations make sense so let's all be on our guard and make the most of the situation.

Rusty added, "native people in the past on earth were all notional minded. They seem to act on emotions as well as rational thinking."

With everyone satisfied as to their circumstance, Rusty gave instructions to his comrades on duties that needed to be fulfilled at this juncture. Some gathered small dry wood for a fire while others made their little cove more unnoticeable with boughs and branches. Two went forth with weapons to find and retrieve game for food. Berries would be nice and well as a fresh supply of water which is always a good thing on a trek of this nature. In a short time, a small fire was set with small dry twigs. Hot water and tea was tenuously provided by Whisper who had kept some for such a situation. The two hunters returned noiselessly with a fat bird for roasting. The camp thus assembled and in order so that all enjoyed some tea and roasted chicken-like bird. Water was found close by so they filled up the canteens. All was well when sleep over took the tired travelers. Guard duty was given to four to keep watch in two-hour intervals. Two on and the two off just to be safe. Four more would be utilized for guard duty later.

Large animals were known in this area according to the Mawpics. Maybe carnivores. They learned that some small bands of roaming robbers could be encountered. Bristle warned of possible bands of young toughs wanting make a name for themselves by decimating the humans. With all these bases covered the night concluded without incident. It was the next few days that would be filled with incidents.

In the morning, it was decided that breakfast would have to wait a few hours so that more distance could be purchased from the indigenous tribes in the lake valley. The winds began to pick up as the atmosphere became heavy with vapors from an unknown source. It took only a short time to ascertain the vapors were from burning vegetation in the region. The winds were strong as was the odor of the burning plants and grasses.

"What is going on?" Whisper and Joel asked no one in particular in unison.

"I am thinking someone has set fire to the undergrowth along the trail to thwart our advancement. It is only a guess," replied Rusty.

The others were thinking the same thing as several small animals crossed the trail in utter terror.

"Bristle Fume was correct when he told me to watch our back and to avoid the obvious trails as the Kampacs had a contingent of young toughs that had vowed to rid the area of the strangers before they had established a foot hold in this region." Rusty finished speaking with gestures towards the smoke and trail.

"The let's heed his advice and move out in a different pattern and get up the trail and back to our friends without delay," replied Joel.

CHAPTER THIRTY-NINE

The smoke continued to fill the air as the eight colonists cautiously moved up the valley, but on a path far from the established trail. The going was difficult for a little while until they came to a small stream.

"This stream most certainly has its origins up on the plateau, so if we follow it our task will be less arduous than fighting all the underbrush and trees in the thick of this forest."

Joel was in complete agreement with Rusty's observations thereby giving the signal to cross the stream and follow it up the valley. This move also had the effect of leaving the smoke and ash far behind them.

"Now all we have to be aware of is any marauding Kampacs or some large carnivore that might inhabit this area," observed Whisper as she tried to keep up with all her stuff. She had left the camp with all of her new finery and had nothing to change into. It was hard going with robes and finery to moderate her advancement. She had started to perspire even as the day had begun to cool. The stream was winding and heavy with much vegetation that was not foreseen when they had first begun to follow it.

Joel had told two of his comrades to be on the lookout for game as well as any miscreants. The stream provided water as well and lunch. The two men looking for food stopped and fished the stream for something to eat as it was past breakfast time. To their delighted surprise, they quickly caught several fish that looked like trout.

Seeking a secluded spot back from the stream and among some great rocks, a fire of small dry twigs was made to cook the fish over the flames. Smoke was barely noticeable. This small portion and some of yesterday's woodsy chicken, washed down with cold water made up a breakfast that must sustain them under dinnertime. Fruit was picked up from time to time as they moved on.

The consensus was reached by discussion that they should return to the main plateau trail since they believed that the fire and miscreants were left far behind. The stream was meandering and presented waterfalls and rapids that made the ascent very difficult going. Huge boulders to move around caused several travelers bruised and sore body parts. With much relief, they all returned to the main trail and easier climbing.

Occasionally the trekkers experienced, when they gained a little hollow, that the air was cool and when back on the evenness of the trail the air was much warmer. The winds blew colder as the day wore on. The area they were now on was rocky and the path sandy. The rocks or boulders loomed up as surprises even though they ranged in size from land car to house dimensions. Any one of these monoliths might hide a contingent of malcontents. Joel had volunteered to be first in the column to search out any dangerous possibilities.

The day wore on as they climbed higher up the slope towards the targeted plateau. The rocks in the path caused the feet to become sore as ankles were tested to the limit. As night began to bleed all around the group, it was thought by all to stop and make camp even though the lip of the plateau was within a few hours climb. Most agreed that a fresh start in the morning would be best for all concerned.

A niche was found not far from the trail with a rock ledge overhang. Because of the threat of rain, this was a most ideal location. Rain clouds and wind had been gathering all day, threatening some inclement weather. This seemed unusual for fine weather had accompanied the settlers for many days. This sudden change caught the trekkers slightly off guard. Dry wood was hard to find as the rain began suddenly without warning.

All eight people barely fit into the protected niche but it was much better than the cold downpour. Some dry wood was found in and around the overhang. Joel and Dirk started a fire by flint and steel that the Mawpics had demonstrated to the colonists. Soon a warm but friendly fire was blazing to ward off the cold and with care each person could move about the niche with ease. The men removed some large rocks from the back of the overhang to facilitate some space to recline, placing the boulders at the entrance of the niche. This made the space even cozier. Dinner was meager for eight hungry travelers. Water from their canteens and some dried fish saved from the Mawpic's camp. A rabbit caught during the day, was roasted over the fire to perfection.

Garner Trapp, Joel, and Dirk had formed a special bond and gravitated to each other in conversation and camaraderie. This had a tenacity to make the group into two factions. This was not detrimental to the whole but was noticeable to Rusty and Whisper. They made every effort to thwart any cliques and were successful by moving into and around each faction with witty conversation as well as challenging them for the next day's happenings.

When the fire died down and the rain and wind abated somewhat, the trekkers, all found a space to curl up and sleep. The day's hike had brought all of them to a type of exhaustion that demanded sleep and rest. Dirk volunteered to take the first watch and would wake Victor after several hours to take the next watch. It probably was not necessary this close to home but it was not the time to take unnecessary chances, opined the group. The night grew cold, rainy, windy, and just plain inhospitable, so much so that most did not sleep well. Trying to turn and rearrange positions, a never-ending activity to keep warm. In the morning, the trekkers were sleepy and slightly irritable from lack of sleep. This caused a division to raise its ugly head. It was decided that the group would divide into two. This was for safety and to return in the same group that had earlier ventured forth. This would give each quartet a full welcome from the colonists on the plateau. Rusty and his original group would head out first and would be followed by Victor and his three comrades. If danger appeared its ugly head when the first group approached it would leave four to follow to render assistance. This was agreeable by all by a vote of confidence and friendliness.

Rusty moved out after another meager breakfast to the congenial goodbyes and good wishes from the remaining group. These four trekkers were very anxious to get back to their loved ones so the group moved out at a swift pace, leaving the others to police the camp and pack up at a leisurely rate. Victor and Whisper worked side by side and quietly discussed the situation.

"I am certain this splitting of the group was a good idea but did Rusty have a deeper and more plausible reason to have suggested this?"

"Well, Whisper I still has an uneasy feeling about this whole event. I can't put my finger on anything in particular, it but its just one of those things that space pilots get occasionally."

Rusty was moving with real purpose in his advance. He continued a dialogue to those that followed on his heals.

"I can't pin point this feeling, it is just a general feeling that something just doesn't seem to be at peace with all of us. It's that feeling you get when close to the edge of a great abyss and yet you are keeping to the trail. A feeling of something pulling you closer to the edge and calamity. It's hard to explain."

"I trust you Rusty, and I will be more diligent that every before, not only for our sakes but for all the colonists," said Garner

After a prescribed interval of time, the remaining four finished their chores and set out to gain the plateau before dark. As the four trekked, they soon left behind the cold and damp condition that had gripped them during the night. The going became more difficult as the trail became steeper as they were getting close to the lip of the great plateau.

Victor was quick and generous with his feelings of dread as they neared this point, so much like Rusty's.

"I just don't like this feeling of impending doom or tragedy. I felt this way once when on night patrol in an uncharted galaxy, when out of the blackness of space came a dozen fighter craft of unknown origins. We fought them off valiantly but came away bruised pretty badly. We never found out who they were but that same feeling is now creeping into my bones and marrow."

The others were in sympathy with Victor and inquired what he would have them do.

Whisper spoke up in her very concerned voice.

"We respect this premonition of yours and will respond as best we can to any suggestions you have about entering the village. You have me thinking about all of this so that I have some misgivings about this entering the colony without some reconnoitering first. What do you suggest we do?

"Mostly, I suggest, we enter the village from the backside by twos in the most secretive way we know how to do. This should eliminate any surprises. According to Victor's suggestion, they split up and stealthily entered into the compound. To their surprise, the area was deserted. Calling, with no response, gave the four the willies. They had hoped Rusty and his group at least would respond. They huddled together in the center of the village trying to determine what had happened to their comrades. It looked as though a calamity had happened in only seconds. Tools and supplies lay about in a manner suggesting sudden surprise. Only Fairly uttered some words.

"What could possibly happen to us next?"

Victor threw up his arms in mock resignation to emphasize his perplexity.

"What would you suggest Fairly?"

"Well what ever has happened here, we must be on guard with our weapons in case the cause is of a threatening nature. Even our four comrades of the deep are gone."

Just as Victor had finished speaking and before weapons were raised and readied a deep and booming voice came from behind one of the huts.

"Well people, I see you have returned to the little gaggle of insurgents. We have been waiting for you to arrive to make this colony of mine complete. You can join or rebel as has Mr. Rusty and his spouse. Other deserting cronies will be treated in a like manner. They of course are in the stockade. Whisper, I want you to come away from that riff-raff that beguiled you into errant behavior."

Battle Winslet was at his most callous self as Waver, Porc, and a few other lackeys backed him up with drawn weapons. "Well! What are you going to do? I haven't all day for you four to decide whether you are joining our colony or spending time in the stockade or possibly dying on the spot."

For a moment, Whisper did not move a muscle or say anything. Into the silence, her voice sped towards her father like an arrow with ferocity that was most uncharacteristic of the young woman.

"Father, you are a fool of magnificent proportions. These people are so attuned to the things of a democratic colony it would be a huge mistake not to take their advice and agree to a democratic form of ruling our established village. Your actions will be duly recorded and punished eventually. Just drop your airs of superiority and let us all work towards a community that will prosper. We don't need you as our ruler."

"Now daughter I feel you have been brainwashed by these miscreants so I will excuse your little tirade. However, I am glad to hear you agree with me as I have elected myself high chief and governor of this New Hope colony. Waver is my vice-Mayor in charge of vice and other forms of gaiety. Your mother is in charge of all village services and activities. Proc is my sergeant of arms to help keep peace and tranquility throughout the entire colony. Now all those that wish to continue under my leadership please raise your hand as agreeing."

No one raised their hand including Whisper. The old counselor looked puzzled and slightly hurt by the response. Everyone on the scene held their breath waiting for the old warrior to explode or vent some new venomous anger at the original residents. He surprised all by declaring that those in a mutinous mode would be escorted to the brig to join the other recently confined mutineers.

Battle's lackeys escorted the four explorers to the brig, hastily enlarged in their absence by the newly arrived interlopers. It was a joyous reunion by Victor's group and Rusty Bolt's loyal people. After a round of hugs and hand clasping, Garner, Joel, Victor and Rusty huddled together to begin to assess the situation.

"How did that old windbag get to our village and take over," said Joel with a wink at Bert indicating in a jovial way that his friend might have lost his touch with security.

Bert answered with a slight guiltiness in his voice.

"The old boy contacted us several times to complain about his circumstances. He was able to use some triangulation to locate our signal, thereby coming on to us at night when we were most vulnerable. He and his troop swooped down on us with weapons and threats. We surrendered so no one was hurt and so far, none of our group has capitulated, that is why it is so crowded in here. We are more than them and I think many of his gang are really fed up with his antics and would welcome a coup de grace. Especially Walter and Carl. A take over by us would be accepted by most of his crew. We could then try to rehabilitate Battle for Whisper and Blenda's sake. I think we must wait a few days to determine the effectiveness of their surveillances and strike when we see any lax in their security."

All in the brig gave unanimous affirmation. The next few days would be difficult for the group because there was so much energy in the group that some worried about a breakout before all the facts were in place, causing a failure.

And so it was. The prisoners were a model of decorum, but carefully watching every move the interloper guards made.

CHAPTER FORTY

After a few restless days with Battle's constant haranguing, the prisoners began to formulate a plan of escape and a return to democratic rule. They determined the numbers that would be loyal to Battle and the number that would be likely to leave his maniacal rule. The conclusion was certainly in their favor, so plans were made to overthrow Battle and his few cronies. Only Whisper inserted an addendum to the plans.

"Please no killing or maiming. Remember, he still is my father and the husband of my very compliant, loving mother."

With this caution in mind, the men of the brig gathered in a corner and began to fine-tune their plan. With quiet but agreeable utterances, the men came to a plan of action. Some of the women not to be left out also gave some good advice and consent. The strategy was one of surprise and cunning. Whisper would complain of sickness and request to see her mother. Whisper was certain her mother would help. This would entail one guard to leave his post accompanying Whisper with only one guard remaining. With only one guard left, it would be easy to break out, overpowering the one incompetent stooge left behind. Joel, Bert, Victor, and Rusty would rush the door with all their combined weight and subdue the one remaining guard. This would be done only after some signal from Whisper that she had obtained a weapon of some sort. With it, they could wake the camp after confining the few leaders of the old insurrection. Mainly Battle, Waver, and Porc.

One very dark and hot night the colonists put the plan into action. Whisper feigned some sort of sickness that worried the guards. Knowing she was Battle's daughter one of them immediately removed her from the brig and assisted her to Blenda's abode as Whisper had requested. After about a half hour the prisoners saw a flashing light coming from Blenda's cabin. With that signal, the four reselected men rushed the door and quickly overpowered the remaining guard. Whisper then came running back to her comrades waving two stun guns above her head. Rusty and Bert took the weapons and speedily but stealthily moved towards Battle's billet where he and Waver and Porc had been staying. It was all over in matter of minutes. The three ringleaders were captured by the breakout group and put under arrest. All of the other members of Battle's original members sided immediately with Rusty Bolt and the original colonist here on the plateau.

When the three miscreants were confined to the repaired brig, the rest of the colony continued with the elemental functions of the village. This was done by drafting a constitution and voting for judges and representatives of the village. Rusty was the president. A three-judge panel would resolve disputes. The representatives were a small group that was tasked with drafting new rules and regulations. The entire process seemed mundane and elementary therefore all participated to make it very practical and complete.

During this time, the brig got only cursory attention. Under this lax situation, it was learned that Waver had beat up his father to the point the old warrior needed hospitalization. Waver and Porc were both involved in this altercation. Both young men seemed subdued after this event. Battle was quite a while in rehabilitation and when fully restored he was a changed man. As Blenda and Whisper nursed Battle back to health, they noticed him declaring all was over, and vanity. He was making it known that he wanted to retire and raise a garden and hoped for grandchildren. Some of this rambling by Battle was taken with a grain of salt. His sincerity was demonstrated by a number of events. One of which was when he noticed his guards had left him unattended, he strolled around the compound until he found someone in authority to remedy the situation. What he didn't know that this scene was played out by Rusty's plan and permission to test Battle's new found nature? This confirmed the entire colony to permit Battle to resume his place as father and husband. The village prospered and slipped in a routine that would insure a new beginning at New Hope.

The Mawpics returning to the plateau complemented this. Waver and Porc were permitted some freedom after promising not to cause any trouble. This permitted some fraternization with the Mawpics and their buddy Bristle Fume and his new wife. This turn of events permitted the boys to stay with the Mawpics more and more. It wasn't long before it was announced by the boys they had found a permanent place with the indigenous people. It was only a matter of time when both young men were betrothed to Mawpic girls, to the joy of Battle and Blenda. This was accentuated by the announcement of Whisper and Bert's engagement. This event had been predicted by everyone and was a culmination of a very wonderful courtship. This gave the new colony and even the planet a definite positive beginning. New Hope was living up to its name. Whisper's final comment about the entire situation, "I can see that this new start is better than a dream. You can have your cake and eat too."

THE END

AN OBSERVATION

The fact that native people have a mistrust of new trespassers on land that had

been loved and enjoyed for years and years seemed to be natural, in this case, familiarity was the condition of acceptance. Kindness and mutual respect played a real part in the Mawpics accepting the humans. In this story. Staying impartial also played a role in the integrating of two different species. Bert and Whisper represented the ideal couple for marriage and lasting companionship. Rusty and Evie played to intelligence and stability. Joel and Gloria acted as helpers and agreeing when needed for a successful endeavor.

This story for me is more of the real account of colonizing a new planet. The big gruesome animals and ugly peoples of some sci-fi accounts seemed very unrealistic to me. Three eyed creatures with fangs and unsightly appendages moved only some to encourage fear in the unknown. I hope some reads this and begins to realize the future possibilities to conquer space. Let us all hope that constraint on earth will not force us to have to venture too far out in the great void of space. God has given us a real utopia if we just learn to utilize our strengths and minimize our faults. We can have our own NEW HOPE.

FINIS

BIO of R.Evans.Pansing

Born 8/19/33
Married 55 years
Associate Pastor 28 years
Love of travel visiting 35 countries.
Hobbies= Painting, fishing, hunting, writing, gardening, refinishing old furniture, Volunteering at Habitat for Humanity in 5 states and three countries.
Three children and several grandchildren.
Enjoying retirement on my 10-acre homestead.
Making good choices early in life have benefited me to live the good life for years.